D0190532

Fables
for the
Clarinet

By Steve Pastis

DEDICATION

This book is dedicated to April, my love, my wife,
and my reason.

This book is also dedicated to the other real life folks who inspired
its characters, some who will recognize themselves and others who
(I hope) won't.

FOREWORD

It's not as if Steve is anything like his stories. He has always seemed quite normal to me when we've met at Mental Conventions over the years. True, I may not be the greatest judge of normalcy in the world, but I'm the best you've got at the moment. He and I share a proclivity for fudging the imagined distinctions between rabbits and men and we each have a liking for worlds unburdened by exact dimensions. So it's understandable that I'm here to recommend this wonderful and strange book.

I would hope you'd read the stories carefully, perhaps limiting yourself to no more than ten a day, taking a day off here and there and watching yourself closely for signs of drifting, meandering, laughing, and the like. If you feel fine, increase your reading. If drifting, etc., cut back to five or so a day, drink lots of water and, if symptoms persist, consult a raccoon.

So there you go. You're on your own now. And remember, asking the author for strict linearity is like asking Thomas Edison to pay for donuts.

Unlikely.

-- Phil Austin

ACKNOWLEDGMENTS

I remember sitting in Miss Fenner's English class at San Marino High School during the 1971-72 schoolyear (in the days when a woman's marital status was announced before her name), wishing I could somehow write as well as some of the other students. When they read their stories aloud, I was in awe and, truth be told, rather jealous.

I tried writing fiction as I was instructed, but never managed to create anything I was happy with – anything that compared to what some of the other students were writing in their senior year of high school.

Sometime during the summer between high school and college, however, all that changed.

My cousin Nick Tripodes showed me some of the short stories he had written in his spare time. He didn't seem to worry about any of the rules that a good high school English teacher insisted her students follow. His stories went into whatever directions he wanted to take them.

I was inspired. From that point on, I would write short stories that went into whatever directions I wanted to take them. It has now been 46 years since I started writing short stories using the Nick Tripodes Method.

And I am happy with them. I may be the only one who is happy with some of these offerings, but I am happy with them nonetheless.

Thank you Nick. We miss you.

I would like to offer special thanks to Phil Austin of Firesign Theatre fame who wrote the foreword for this short story collection. He passed away in 2015 and is missed by countless Firesign Theatre fans.

By including the foreword that he was kind enough to write, I am admitting that the book you reading has been "in production" for many years. Even so, I really wanted to include it because the Firesign Theatre has been one of the major influences on my writing.

My thanks also to Marilyn Scott-Waters who designed the cover for this book way back in 2001. (As previously confessed, this book is the result of a very long process.)

Special thanks also to my editor, Nita Congress, who had the tough task of editing quirky stories that often create their own rules.

And a sincere thank you – this one with a lot of love – to my dear wife, April, who has offered encouragement and been my main audience for many years, for taking my ramblings and ideas and somehow creating a real book out of them.

-- Steve Pastis

ABOUT SOME OF THE STORIES

"Something Like a Raccoon Called Duluth on the Maxwells' Phone" appeared in *Signs of Life: Channelsurfing through '90s Culture*, edited by Jennifer Joseph and Lisa Taplin; a few years later, "Something Like a Raccoon Called Duluth on the Maxwells' Phone" appeared in *Voices of Hellenism*, Vol. 1, No. 1; "Wet Dogs of Hispaniola," "The Bucket Seats of Poets," and "The Zesty Saints" were published in *Gargoyle #55*, edited by Richard Peabody; "The Antithesis of Margaret (In Eight Phases)" appeared in *Voices of Hellenism*, Vol. 1, No. 3; and "Ask Wisconsin/The Oncoming Bureau of Longitudes" was included in *Offbeat/Quirky (Journal of Experimental Fiction, Volume 73)*, edited by Eckhard Gerdes. Several of the stories in this book appeared in newsletters of organizations Steve belonged to at the time. He forgets which ones.

Something Like a Raccoon Called Duluth on the Maxwells' Phone

It was a raccoon that broke into the Maxwells' home and ran up their telephone bill to an astronomical amount. Or so they told the lemon-scented woman at the counter of the telephone office.

"Really and truly, that's the way it occurred," maintained Mr. Maxwell, the brains of the family. "We don't know anybody in Duluth."

Mrs. Maxwell nodded, as did the three young Maxwells. The woman at the counter walked off in the general direction of her immediate supervisor. She decided to pass this problem along to someone paid to handle such things.

Selma was the supervisor at the office that day. She knew enough to find the Maxwell file and take it with her to the front counter and the waiting Maxwells.

"I find the story about the raccoon hard to believe," Selma told the Maxwell clan. "It says here that two months ago you claimed that $430 in phone bills was attributed to a buffalo that snuck in through your kitchen window and called his brother in the Antelope Valley. December of last year, you claimed that an antelope had knocked down your front door to make eight hours of calls to his nephew in Buffalo. And now this raccoon. How stupid do you think we are?"

Mr. and Mrs. Maxwell speculated on the stupidity level of the phone company staff without reaching an appropriate conclusion. The discussion returned to the raccoon situation after about five minutes.

"A raccoon could not have broken in your house and used the phone," explained Selma. "A raccoon would have immersed the telephone in water before having anything to do with it. The water would have rendered the telephone useless. Instead of a high phone bill, you people would be bringing in the telephone for repairs."

Mr. Maxwell thought for a moment.

"A badger! That's it! It was a badger that broke into our home and called Duluth," said the patriarch of the Maxwell family.

Selma thought for a moment and signed an approval for a refund for the calls to Duluth. The Maxwells were happy and went home. They were greeted by a mountain lion who was sitting in their kitchen talking to relatives in Saginaw.

"What do we do now?" asked one of the younger Maxwells of her equally concerned father. He thought for some time before bringing out his camera. A photograph might be needed for their next visit to the telephone company counter.

"Some people are so suspicious," Mr. Maxwell thought to himself.

The photographs of the mountain lion came out so well that extra copies were sent to several magazines. The money the magazines paid for the photos was used by the Maxwells to install bars on all the windows and extra locks on all of the doors.

After that, any animals wanting to use the Maxwells' telephone had to resort to extreme cleverness to get into the house. They would dress up as Girl Scouts selling cookies or more often as telephone repairmen. The Maxwells were pretty sharp and always seemed to be one step ahead of these would-be long distance telephone call makers.

One day, a reporter came by to do a story about the struggle of the Maxwell family against the members of the animal kingdom that sought to run up their telephone bills. Once inside the house, the reporter was attacked by the Maxwell clan who mistakenly thought he was a lynx. The entire Maxwell family was sent to prison for the attack.

These days, the members of the animal kingdom are free to use the Maxwell telephone for calls to anywhere they want. No Maxwells are there to defend their home, but no animals come around. Somehow, it's not fun anymore.

Wired Like Potomac Trout

McKensey said his good-byes to the laundress and her remaining guests before walking directly into the entry closet, something he had a habit of doing. He didn't smoke, drink, or swear, and wild sex was usually out of the question. His thing was walking into closets.

McKensey would be at a party or even a family gathering and, unless someone took him by the hand and led him out the front door, he would invariably wind up in the closet. His friends or family would look at each other and nod – as if from a scene on *Dragnet* – and a moment or two later someone would open the door to the closet and help him out. He would be rather red-faced as he made his apologies, but unless he had help, he was back in the closet after the next round of good-byes.

From this night on, however, things would be different. The laundress knew all about his problem and took the time to find a solution for McKensey. The third time he was assisted from the entry closet, the laundress took his hand and led him to the back patio to talk for a while.

"I have done some research on this problem of yours, McKensey," said the laundress helpfully and very, very diplomatically. "Regrettably, the local library has little information on your problem. I called a few friends who are either psychiatrists or need them, or both, but they too were of little help."

McKensey remained silent as he took in every word. Perhaps the laundress could really help him from being embarrassed by his problem in the future.

"Wait here for a moment," she said and hurried into the house. Back a minute later, the laundress held a small paper bag.

"I am afraid that you are being invited to less and less parties because of your problem," the laundress said frankly. "Hosts and hostesses are embarrassed for you and they hate having a party end with that feeling. I have here in this bag a solution to your problem."

The laundress pulled out a small tape recorder and set it on the wrought iron table between them. She turned the recorder on. Four types of sounds were heard: a toilet flushing, a telephone ringing, the sounds of an elevator, and the voices of giggling women saying "Oooh, McKensey!"

"All you have to do is play this tape whenever you find yourself in a closet and people will think you are clever, instead of a flaming toad," explained the laundress.

McKensey took the tape recorder, thanked the laundress profusely, and walked into the house. The laundress arose slowly and entered the house in time to hear the last of McKensey's fourth series of good-byes. She watched as once again he walked into the closet.

This time, however, she heard the sound of the toilet flushing from inside the closet and McKensey emerged without help. He was greeted by appreciative laughter as he pretended to buckle his belt.

"McKensey, it slipped my mind, but we're having a party next week and we forgot to invite you," said one of the other departing guests. The statement wasn't quite true since they had not mentioned the party to McKensey on purpose. But if he was this funny to have around, maybe he did deserve an invitation after all.

The laundress smiled at McKensey and led him by the hand out the front door in an effort to have him save as much of the tape as possible. Her plan seemed to be working and as it happened, it worked even better at the next party. The people by that front door loved the sound of the telephone as once again McKensey wound up in the front closet.

This time, however, he was not helped out of the house, so soon he was back in the closet. The sound of women moaning and giggling from the closet went over very well. McKensey had thought ahead and brought some lipstick and learned how to apply it to his hand in such a way that after pressing his hand to his face, the result looked like a female kiss. He was able to apply several to his face very effectively, even in the dark.

This time the laughter was much louder than before. McKensey received invitations for parties for the next five Friday nights. He was euphoric. He also was back in the closet. No problem, the sounds of the elevator went over very well and the laughter continued for quite a while.

He was helped out the front door by a couple of women and McKensey was in his glory. The two women even competed to take him home. The smile on his face lasted for days.

Six days, to be precise. At that point, he realized that he had used up all four of the sounds on the tape the laundress had given him. He called her up and asked her if she could supply him with any more sounds.

The laundress had anticipated this moment and had created several new sounds on a new tape. Things had changed somewhat since her party, however. The laundry business had fallen on hard times as more people began washing their own clothes. The laundress wanted to be a good friend to McKensey, but she needed to start making money for her troubles. She asked him for $100 for the tape.

"You're trying to take advantage of our friendship," said an angry McKensey to a startled laundress. As she saw the situation, it was he who was attempting to get her efforts for nothing.

"It's $100 or no tape," she stated bluntly.

He hung up. Certainly with his creativity he could make his own tape. He knew he had been able to successfully embellish the first tape to get the maximum laughter from it. He was also very self-confident – perhaps even overconfident because of the romantic efforts of the two women from the second party who continued to compete for his attentions.

He held his tape recorder in one hand as he flipped his channel changer in hopes of finding some noises to use for his trips into the closet at the party the next night. Staying up until three a.m., he finally had his work completed.

At the Barnes' party the next night, McKensey decided to "leave" early. A crowd gathered around the entry closet to hear the sounds from the closet. The sound of a river flowing was heard and out of the closet strolled McKensey with a fish in his coat pocket and a fishing line around his waist.

"Look at me," he said to a puzzled group, "I'm wired like Potomac trout."

There were a few glances among and between the other partygoers. A snicker was heard, and then it happened. Laughter. Uproarious laughter. Those around the closet may not have understood what they were laughing about but they were laughing just the same.

There was a pause and the group looked around for McKensey. He was back in the closet. They were silent in anxious anticipation. The sound of tap dancing was heard and then a loud crash. McKensey emerged from the closet in a sequined skirt and with an automobile tire around his head.

"Did you see which way the man in the balcony went?" said McKensey as he did a classic double-take. Those by the closet were in hysterics.

It was fortunate that every single person waiting for him to emerge from the closet expected him to be hilarious. If he had to establish himself with what he presented that night, he would have attended his last party.

But McKensey had successfully established himself before that night and could now get away with anything, and sooner or later he would. These were the basic rules of show business.

All the Rage

Carmen sneezed into the tray of anchovies. A faux pas had been committed and she cringed at what she had done. A moment was spent considering her next move.

"To sneeze into the anchovies is real big on the continent," she announced to her fellow guests and curious hosts. "It's all the rage, I assure you."

A line formed in front of the anchovies. A new trend needed to be explored. The guests would test the merits of what they had been told "was all the rage." A few were deep in concentration, trying to summon a sneeze to be ready when it was their turn at the front of the line.

The hosts of the party were puzzled. This was most certainly not the way they had planned the evening. They had other things in mind when they called the society page writers and photographers to be in attendance. This was the party that would make them somebodies.

"My God! The reporters!" thought Mrs. Bacon, the female half of the hosts, loudly to herself. "There must be no photographs taken of any of this."

Unfortunately, it was a tad too late to stop the press. Flashbulbs captured the sneezes on film before either of the Bacons reacted. A group shot of the opera singer from Wisconsin, the congressman for the district, a distinguished architect, and two young widows (who were well-provided for) were gangsneezing into the anchovy tray. And this would be the lead picture on page 3 of the fourth section of the local newspaper!

Mr. Bacon knew that embarrassment would abound when that issue hit the streets, so he thought quickly. He called over the reporter and told him that his name was Fred Morgan. He said that he and his wife, whose name was Blanche (another fib), thought this was a great party and that sneezing into the anchovies was a worthwhile thing to do. The reporter took down all he said as fact.

As it turned out, there really was a Fred Morgan, and a Blanche Morgan, too. They were the couple that the Bacons wanted to outdo, which is why they held the party in the first place. The Morgans were holding an outdoor barbecue that day and didn't see fit to invite the Bacons. The party was the Bacons' revenge. And if somebody had to look bad in all of this, the Bacons preferred it to be the Morgans.

And so it was that the Morgans looked like fools when their names were listed as hosts for the party with the sneezing into the anchovies. Mr. Bacon got a chuckle out of the newspaper account he read.

That was until he read the story on the next page that showed several of the guests at the Morgans' barbecue improperly and somewhat obscenely using their eating utensils to prod the barbecuing lamb on the spit. One of the guests had convinced the other guests that this sort of prodding was "all the rage on the continent" and it became the thing to do at the barbecue.

The pictures were disgusting. What upset Mr. Bacon more, however, was that he was listed as the host for the barbecue. It seems that an editor realized that the Morgans simply could not host a party and a barbecue at the same time and since he knew that one of the events was a Bacon-hosted event, he attributed the barbecue to the Bacons.

Mr. Bacon sizzled in anger when he realized the chuckles that must be circulating around town because of the newspaper coverage of the barbecue. He contemplated his revenge on the Morgans. Next weekend, he decided, would be a good time for a poolside party that would be announced as a Morgan-hosted social event. He contemplated several disgusting social customs to introduce that could be described as "all the rage" to a gullible batch of guests. He thought about what to do and how to achieve his goal of revenge.

Meanwhile, the social elite of the community thought about how to achieve their immediate goal. They wanted to be on the Bacons' permanent guest list.

Mad Heron of Austin (The Dangerous Pillow)

A mad heron from Austin stood sharpening the corners of a pillow on a bed belonging to strangers. Vengeance drove him on since he recognized some of the feathers as being from one of the fishing chums with whom he had spent a recent winter.

Any questions? Yes, you in the back.

Can a blue jay be declared ambidextrous after being tested by the proper authorities?

The mad heron explained as he continued his work to startle and possibly injure the owners of the pillow, "Many are not as ambidextrous as those celebrating ornithological breakthroughs would have us believe. The champagne often looks too good to delay consuming just to double-check one's notes."

Can I be sure that my finch is pure by taking her word for it?

The mad heron turned to me and tossed the dangerous pillow back in place. "Many questions in life," he explained, "are best left to the flip of a coin. If the result is wrong, spend the coin somewhere unpleasant."

If all is fair in love and war, should I buy a large cat to frighten my oriole into chirping less?

The mad heron flew out the window only to return a minute later with a book he had scratched together for a major publisher. "Third chapter, verses seventeen through twenty," he said, and I read the following:

*A cat is not what ought be bought
to silence the bird with orange blot.
Instead perhaps a better thought
is a pistol held by a deadeye shot.*

How does one cope with the emotional distress of a bird with severe feather loss?

The mad heron thought for a moment and smiled. "Perhaps I have been too hasty," he said and he softened the corners of the pillow, making them not only safe again but even more comfortable than before his visit. "I was about to tell you that encouraging the bird to sell the feathers and buy something he would enjoy is a good way to cope. I was also about to list beer as a good choice of purchase when I realized that is probably what my fishing chum did."

With that he flew out the window to find his friend. A friend becomes dearer after falsely believed lost.

Episode Twelve of 'Hiram the Majestic'

(The story so far: Hiram T.M. has been approached by several tall people to embark on a yearlong voyage across the seven seas. While on his voyage, Hiram's kingdom has been taken over by the tall people. Hiram's family has been banished to somewhere unpleasant, perhaps Indiana, and his castle has been burned to the ground. Hiram's fortunes are not all grim, however. He has acquired some interesting souvenirs and most of the pictures he has taken will become good slides. As Episode Twelve begins, Hiram is sitting in a ship cabin writing some postcards to family and friends.)

HIRAM *(talking to himself as he writes)*: It's been many months since I've seen my family and friends. I miss my kingdom. Alas, I have my voyage to complete and this is a burden that must be endured by someone like me. 'Tis a curse to be this majestic. Lo, a knock at my door. Must be room service. Bye for now. Love, Hiram.

(Stay tuned for Episode Thirteen...)

Rabid at Best (Episode I)

She was rabid at best as the hotel took the blazer and she was adrift with no myth for the ride. She studied the lines of the flood in the static and was awarded some wood, somehow in her size.

The lion meanwhile stood adjusting his shadow so he could do more work than he had done yet. He growled and she heard it and looked out the window and spotted a leopard, which guarded the bank. The leopard, named Henry, had habits unmentioned, a walnut or fable would bring out the cape. She watched as he patted the shine-happy sidewalk and she turned to her beast with his shadow of fear.

"So tell me, dear Oscar," she spoke at the lion, "will wintertime bring me a summit this year? I've pardoned the sad one who scuttled the coffee and hid with a walrus who swallowed his ear."

The lion turned slowly still watching his shadow and looked at the lady who spoke with a leer. He thought about answers and unanswered questions and pondered a public that rattled beer bottles.

"The summit, dear lady, will come like a beagle with blue silhouettes on a channel so clear," the lion continued, ignoring his shadow. "My dear sweet vat of matter, you are wishing too much."

A telegram drew all the motions of moments and reading aloud was permitted by all. She read with division of a last-time marauder who had once shared her shadow when all things were clear. The days had flung hooey since a stroll through the hedges but she well remembered how notions could steer.

"Dear lion," she spoke with a voice on a platter. "Dear lion," she said with heart, drawing him near. "Do you remember a place in a dusting where rabbit shells gathered and Solomon played? This message was sent by a far distant usher who once could remember the way to the stage.

"It seems our departed is still wishing with roses and while rabid at best is still hunting the shade. His message decoded encoded with shutters says simply with blisters, 'He's leaving the trade.'"

The lion turned back to the current wall shadow and she, his dear friend, looked back out to the street. The bank had been moved to a blackstone in Jersey but she could repeat the sounds its shutters made.

Shooting Mallards

Dexter and Lizette were seated in a small boat on a lake as mallard ducks flew by. Lizette stood up and pointed her rifle at the one at the far end of the third neat row. She fired and missed. Dexter breathed a sigh of relief, unfortunately, loud enough for her to hear.

"Whose side are you on?" Lizette asked. "The one of the woman who loves you or the one of those ducks you've never seen before and wouldn't have even known existed if it wasn't for me?"

She tapped her foot in anger, which is a quite an effective attention-getter in a small boat.

"Yours, of course, dearest," Dexter replied slowly. His thoughts focused on what his childhood would have been without Daffy or Donald. Neither one was a mallard, but they were close enough. A question popped into his head, one that he feared asking. This could have serious consequences if he was given the answer he dreaded.

"Dearest, what other animals do you like to shoot?" Dexter asked, carefully having edited out the word "defenseless."

"Bears," said Lizette, as she thought for a moment about other animals. During that moment, Dexter looked pale as he considered the deaths of Yogi, Boo-Boo, and the grouchy bear that could never get to hibernate for one reason or another in old cartoons.

"Tigers," said Lizette to test Dexter's facial response. He pictured bowls of Sugar Frosted Flakes being orphaned.

"Lions," she said and he thought about a cartoon character or two before it occurred to him that she was putting him on.

"Dexter, did I tell you that I ran over a cat last night?" she said in a soft tone, again catching him off guard. Through Dexter's mind ran images of Jinx, Sylvester... oh no, what was next.

"I had my dog put to sleep because it bit me," Lizette said. She saw Dexter whisper the name "Huckleberry" as his face became even whiter.

"You know what's more fun than shooting mallards?" Lizette asked. Dexter didn't want to hear. No! Change the subject quickly. She was starting to speak again. Think fast Dexter! Think fast!

"Shooting bunnies!" Lizette said and Dexter nearly fainted. "Not Bugs," he thought. This was too cruel.

Lizette started laughing and it took Dexter some time to understand that she had been teasing him all along. Soon, the color returned to his face.

"You know what's even more fun than shooting rabbits?" Lizette asked. Dexter remained relatively calm this time. He had been through the worst of it. She had mentioned the potential demise of Bugs too quickly to make anything afterward effective.

"Being in love with you, Dexter," she said in his favorite voice. Dexter smiled. He would do his best to keep her in love with him. Not just for himself, but for his friends in the animal kingdom.

They took a walk along the shore later in the day, where they found a hot dog stand. Dexter bought the hot dogs and they ate as they looked out over the water where more mallards flew by.

Lizette smiled to herself as her mind wandered to what she and Dexter were eating. For a moment, but only a brief one, she considered talking about Porky and Petunia.

Odd Zed's Planet

The red clarion was in full force as the zenith approached the incompetent winds. Springtime was in demand on the calendar of Odd Zed's planet but beneath the sheaths were shades of negative welcome mats. Another approach beckoned those to survey the system while more Buicks drove by.

Desperation was unlimited from the front to the back of the sudden whispers. Someone could have been a driver that summer but the swooning was deliberately misplanted. Odd Zed knew his place and that was in the Room of Yesterday. It could have been a twilight that attracted the moths but only a tall regent can please the white walls of free thinkers. And more Buicks drove by.

Arnold's World

Arnold looked through the curtain at the caterpillars that were filling up the auditorium for his talk on the advantages of learning a foreign language. This was not the crowd he had hoped for.

He started to drift off in his imaginary world where all was pleasant and smelled good. How he wished he had taken the advice of the tree people and become taller. In his dreams, he had taken that path. In his dreams, he was taller.

An earthquake shook the building and the roof caved in. The caterpillars that were gathered in anticipation of expanding their linguistic horizons were instead expanded horizontally into linguini.

Arnold pictured himself riding along the beach wearing clothes that were in style. The tie he imagined himself wearing was exactly the right width according to the most current of trends. People would come up to him, measure the width of his tie, and give him their admiration and respect. Life smelled good and he was even taller.

He awoke in a hospital as the only survivor of the auditorium roof collapse. He had been wedged in between two beams, which protected him from the falling rubble. Better news for Arnold was that he had been wedged in with such pressure that he was taller.

There were flowers in his hospital room that made him happy. The world that he was temporarily confined to smelled good. All was right in Arnold's world.

Selma's Hope

Selma stood tall, walked proudly and asked the man in the next car for a sixteen-ounce can of beer. Horns honked. People craned their necks out of car windows to learn the reason they were not progressing forward on an apparently green light.

She got back into her car without a can of beer. She pouted. "There are other streets and other cars," she thought. "There is always hope."

A few minutes later, she drove over to the liquor store, conceding defeat. "I'll just have to break down and pay for one myself," she decided.

Hope faded fast in Selma's life.

The Antithesis of Margaret (in Eight Phases)

PHASE ONE: Introduction to the Problem

The antithesis of Margaret had just entered the room. We all thought that Margaret had decided to leave us. In reality, she was still with us, smoking a Winston 100.

PHASE TWO: A Plot Development

One of the two opposite beings (Margaret or her antithesis) had begun reading Dutch poetry from a blue piece of paper. The words seemed melodic, but not being able to see who was speaking was really disturbing to us.

PHASE THREE: A Clarification

The poetry was not original Dutch work but rather translations of American favorites.

PHASE FOUR: A Rude Awakening to Some of Us

Margaret realized that the presence of her antithesis had canceled her from our sight. She scampered around the room doing unpleasant things to us to let us know she was still around.

PHASE FIVE: A Further Complication

Another person, a gentleman in his late fifties, entered the room unaware of the situation.

PHASE SIX: A Partial Resolution to the Situation

Realizing that he knew none of us, the gentleman who had just entered the room smiled to us and left.

PHASE SEVEN: The Final Resolution to Our Dilemma

Margaret was saved when her antithesis left the room briefly to powder her nose. Upon being able to see Margaret once again, we grabbed her by the arm and quickly departed.

PHASE EIGHT: The Epilogue

Margaret is currently married to a bowling alley manager in Canton, Ohio. The rest of us have gone our separate ways.

The Tune Went through Daniel

The tune went through Daniel like a record playing itself out of style. "I'm afraid I've forgotten it," he admitted.

Mr. Welbert was not used to people forgetting melodies, not in his studio, not on his time. "I have had people fired for forgetting a single note, but since you are only here to deliver the pizza, I'll settle for not paying my bill."

Daniel, relieved, mumbled a "fair enough" as he turned and left the studio.

Buchanan Gets Change for a Dollar

Buchanan walked to the drug store. "Change for a dollar, please," he said to the timeworn face behind the counter. "I was a boy here," he added.

More trouble lurked in wait for Buchanan as he made his way to the phone booth across the street. It wasn't enough to have car trouble but in the reflection of the telephone booth chrome, he saw that he had worn a tie that was no longer in style. "Life can be so cruel," he thought.

Later that day, however, he bought a new tie and now lives happily in another community.

Ghastly as Well as Can Be Remembered

"Okay, you win this time around," decided Horace. "Your second grade teacher was much grislier than mine. Let's try the people behind the counter where we each usually bought our childhood candy."

"Can we use ghastliness as the yardstick this time around?" inquired Nathaniel, who continued only after Horace nodded. "Mrs. Crompers was definitely ghastly."

Fearing a second-straight defeat, Horace needed to use some strategy. He had unfortunately nodded his head in agreement too quickly when Nathaniel suggested ghastliness as a category. He really hadn't expected him to have the edge in both grisly second grade teachers and ghastly candy-counterpeople. By their rules, however, he couldn't withdraw his nod.

And the Mr. Walters in his childhood remembrances was more gruesome than ghastly. Horace and his fellow kids never let Mr. Walters put their candy into a bag. That would mean he would actually *touch* the wrappers of what they had intended to eat. And he was gruesome. Sort of ghastly too, but apparently not as much as this Mrs. Crompers person.

But Horace had a plan...

"Nathaniel, I have this feeling that you were a mere child when you were only a kid," Horace said slowly and slyly. He made a fist and yelled "All right!" when Nathaniel nodded. Then he proceeded to Phase Two...

"Adults were much more fearsome then, weren't they?" proceeded Horace. Another Nathaniel nod and Horace continued, "And there was a time when sweet little old ladies were feared by us, wasn't there?"

Another nod was issued and Horace went for the whole enchilada.

"You may have this ghastly picture of Mrs. Crompers deeply embedded in your childhood memories, but isn't it possible that she may have been a sweet little old lady?" Horace inquired with his eyes open wide, waiting for the nod that would signal victory.

"Nope," responded Nathaniel. "The lady was ghastly. Even my parents said she was ghastly and they were old enough to know about such things."

An argument proceeded, not that Horace really had a case. He hoped that somehow Nathaniel would say something unintended – perhaps describing Mrs. Crompers as sweet or wholesome – and Horace would have the momentum needed to win their game of words and memories.

"I'm so sure that Mrs. Crompers is not as ghastly as you remember that I'm willing to drive to your old neighborhood to ask anyone who might remember her to describe her," offered Horace in frustration. "I'll bet you $100 that she really wasn't ghastly."

The two men agreed to the wager but decided to stop for lunch first. Ever since Horace made the decision to go for the whole enchilada in their argument, he wanted to stop for Mexican food. So they did.

They found a Mexican restaurant in Nathaniel's old neighborhood and sat and discussed the requirements of ghastliness while they waited for their order. At the same time, an elderly gentleman came in and took the table beside theirs. The owners knew him and Nathaniel seemed to recognize him also, although he couldn't think of his name.

Nathaniel didn't really want to spend too much time looking at the man because he looked grisly. Possibly gruesome too, but definitely grisly. Nathaniel adjusted his chair so that he could face away from the man with less effort. Horace smiled as a thought occurred to him.

"Nathaniel, I do believe that this gentleman would know ghastly," said Horace suppressing a laugh. He thought about saying that the man's face was the dictionary illustration for "grisly," but he figured Nathaniel got the idea. "I think I will ask him if he knows Mrs. Crompers."

Horace decided to wait until the meal they ordered was safely eaten before facing the man long enough to pose that question. Lunch was delicious and soon over. It became Horace's move.

"Excuse me, sir," Horace said. "Do you know a Mrs. Crompers?"

"Yes," he responded.

"Could you describe her to me?" Horace asked.

"It would be my pleasure," said the old man. "She is a true beauty. Her hair, although grayed by the years, has retained its silky quality. Her eyes are a deep blue, as blue as the clear blue sky. Her lips are still as inviting as when she first moved to this town fifty years ago. Her smile is both innocent and knowing. Many are the times that I have thought about her as I listened to a sweet melody."

Nathaniel was stunned by the man's description of Mrs. Crompers. Could he really have been so wrong about her? Even Horace was startled and he had never even seen the woman.

"She still works at the candy counter at the drug store," continued the man. Horace and Nathaniel were quickly out the door to seek the truth about Mrs. Crompers. The drug store was only three doors away so it wasn't long before the two were standing before the candy counter. They saw the top of a gray head behind the counter as they heard the sound of cardboard boxes being ripped open.

Then she stood up. It was Mrs. Crompers. And, truth be known, she was the ghastliest woman either of them had ever seen. Nathaniel smiled, although he needed to turn away from her. He knew he had won his bet. He waited for the color to return to Horace's face. He also waited for the stockboy to arrive with a mop.

A few minutes later, Nathaniel was helping Horace out of the drug store. The grisly old man who had been in the restaurant was holding the door open for them before going inside.

"Thank you, Mr. Crompers," said Nathaniel automatically, having gained tremendous confidence in his childhood recollections.

Opposing Emperors

Millwad the Bulky was keen on reestablishing the empire his father had lost going for an inside straight. Orostan the Mumbler, meanwhile, overslept and was pushing hard to compensate for the time he lost by not grabbing land in the a.m. The two emperors were clearly on a collision course.

The aspiring emperors were bitter enemies even before they were aware of each other. Their goals were too clashy for them not to hate each other's guts. Before they even met, they prepared to fight each other.

Regrettably, at least for Millwad and Orostan, neither could afford an army. They could only afford to place classified ads to attract soldiers. Although they each received a good number of telephone responses, those calling lost all interest when told that they would be fighting for the honor of Millwad the Bulky or the glory of Orostan the Mumbler. Those calling were hoping instead to be paid, something that neither emperor could manage.

So it came to pass on the day of battle that only two soldiers appeared. One walked from the west, the other strolled in from the east. Alas, the two soldiers were really the two emperors decked out in heavy rented armor suits. By the time they met in the valley, both Millwad and Orostan were bushed from their long walks. Their armor weighed them down more with each step they took until they finally got within shouting distance.

"Can we rest for a while?" asked Millwad the Bulky.

"You know, I sure could use a cold Dr Pepper right about now," mumbled Orostan the Mumbler.

They decided to have a temporary truce that would enable them to walk into the city and get some Dr Pepper. The first place they came to was a bowling alley with a snack bar. They went inside and ordered their cold drinks and watched the bowlers.

Both of the emperors were bowlers, a fact that quickly came up in conversation. They decided to replace their battle with a bowling tournament that would be held that night.

They bowled a game and then another and then another. The score didn't matter in their battle. This was a contest of endurance. They were still at it at four a.m. when they realized that maybe the other wasn't such a bad emperor after all. Millwad was helpful in advising Orostan about how to pick up difficult splits and Orostan let Millwad use his spare towel.

They became friends and decided that it was more fun to go bowling than it was to administer their subjects, especially since they both lived in Kansas. They would never realize that they didn't actually have empires, or that they lived in the greatest country on earth where people freely elect their leaders.

And it's those leaders we look to who will decide what wars we fight and why.

Myron and the Rest of Us
(A Munch to Friendship)

Somehow, Myron wasn't quite as intense as the rest of us. When our gang would get together we would shout things out. Sometimes obscenities, sometimes clean stuff. Myron wouldn't.

A bit more to the odd was Clark.

Clark was tall but he would insist on imitating insects. He would become a different one each week, transforming our group outings into a sort of insect-of-the-week club. Audrey kept on bringing different insect sprays hoping to eventually bring the right one to correspond to Clark's chosen species. One fine May evening, Audrey guessed correctly and brought a box of Snarol. Our gang was one less.

Umbecker wore green socks. I mean really bright green socks. They sort of bugged the rest of us and we would shout out at him. All of us would shout, except of course Myron, who would mumble something in the general direction of the green socks. Audrey, fortunately, guessed right one day and found some poison that worked on people with green socks. Our gang was another one less.

The police eventually caught up with Audrey. She was given forty years to life. Myron left the gang sometime last year. Being so quiet we didn't know he had left until months later.

It seems that I was the last member of our group. We had agreed that whoever was the last member would be the one to open a special bottle of wine and offer a toast to those who had been a part of our little group. The gang never bought the bottle of wine as it had planned and I thought better than to spend my own money so foolishly. I did, however, buy a bag of Fritos and offer a munch to friendship.

Afternoon Incident with Thaddeus & Lulu

The professor continued to put things in a neat row across his desk. Lulu, his top student, seemed especially concerned, even slightly guilty, about the emotional state of the professor. Looking at her, my suspicions were confirmed.

As the professor used his yardstick to perfect the alignment of the various items on his desk, I looked at Lulu again and I pictured her running across a field of dust, her red hair glistening in the gentle spring breeze. That was so long ago — before the stampede and at least a few weeks before Professor Thaddeus.

Lulu walked to the professor and put her hand on his shoulder. She tried to show him all the compassion she could offer, while still keeping the deception she had created for me intact. I wondered why she just didn't admit her relationship to the professor.

I would have let her go easily. She had done so much to help me. Without her I probably wouldn't have survived the crayon panic. Without her, well, I probably would have been the one obsessed with lining up items on my desk.

When she realized that the touch of her hand wasn't enough to help free the professor from his task, she grabbed his hand and pulled him to face her. She kissed and embraced him and looked at me with a "now you know" look.

My heart sank as she tried her best to help the professor. When she left him to approach me and round out the details of her physical admission, the professor immediately went back to his task. He started taking out handfuls of paper clips to incorporate into his grand alignment. Lulu turned to see that her brave actions were in vain.

Leaving me in midsentence, Lulu went back to the professor and inspected the line of items on his desk. She hadn't seen the locket before. She picked it up and opened it.

"Who is this woman, Thad?" she asked politely. He didn't respond to her question. She could have asked him again but the note she picked up between the eraser and the McGovern button seemed to give her the answer she sought.

Lulu walked out of the classroom. I wanted to see the locket — at least until I walked over and actually looked at it. Kathy, my Kathy, had another admirer and God only knows what else.

"So this is why Kathy couldn't come with me to the supermarket opening!" I thought to myself. "This is probably also why she's been wearing turtleneck sweaters."

I was mad at Kathy and the professor, and still very upset with Lulu. I didn't know where Lulu went and I hadn't seen Kathy since the eclipse, but the professor, one of the three sources of my anger, was right there in front of me. I walked up to his desk and scrambled up his neat line. He stared at me and feebly thanked me as he snapped from his daze.

I didn't see Kathy or Lulu until the Eskimo incident and even then I decided not to call either of them again. It took me quite a while to get over the afternoon with the professor and I didn't want to repeat my mistakes when there were so many other new ones to try.

I thought I was doing the right thing. I gave my compassion to two women who needed it, and I even had the wisdom to keep them apart. My good intentions, however, were all wasted. I suppose if you want to have order in any part of your life, it's best to establish it where you can have everything your way, where everything lines up exactly the way you want it.

I decided to take Professor Thaddeus to the university pub for a drink. He is a wise man.

Theories about Beets and Toads and Houston

"There are always reasons for things," Aunt Hildy would tell the woman in the tan convertible. "There's always a reason."

Aunt Hildy would never explain how she knew that there were reasons for things. The woman in the tan convertible always drove off before Aunt Hildy could continue. I was too young to deserve a response to any serious questions, but even then I wondered how she knew there were reasons for everything. I also wondered what those reasons might be. Did Aunt Hildy ever know any of the reasons *anything* was the way it was?

Aunt Hildy learned to drive late in life and she celebrated that accomplishment with a cross-country journey. She was accompanied by her best friend in her later years, a toad named Barnes. It seemed to the young me that she was on a mission of sorts, although I couldn't imagine what that would have been at the time. Every once in a while, I find myself thinking about her trip.

I recall that she told the woman in the tan convertible about her trip the day before she left. I think I heard the woman ask Aunt Hildy why she was going. I know I heard Aunt Hildy respond, "There are always reasons for things."

I still have the three postcards she sent me from her trip. The first was from Tucson and it refers to the purple lights she saw when she looked out her motel window. The second was from El Paso. She took up the entire half of the postcard to complain about beets and how they seemed to affect the minds of the truck drivers who transported them. The third, also from El Paso but postmarked ten days later, only has a generic "miss you" message.

Along with them, I have an unpostmarked letter from a woman named Marie, who apparently met Aunt Hildy somewhere along her journey. She wrote to me to let me know that Aunt Hildy was alright.

"She drove the toad past Houston," she wrote about my aunt. "I was with her as she discussed her theories about beets and toads and Houston. We are now somewhere in Alabama, although Mississippi is a strong possibility. If there was a 'You Are Now in Mississippi' sign, I missed it. There have been trucks driving along both sides of us since we left Mobile. Your Aunt Hildy complains about the trucks but Barnes doesn't seem to mind them at all."

I don't know any more about Marie than her first name and what she wrote in her letter. When Aunt Hildy returned, she was alone. Even Barnes was gone. I asked why Barnes wasn't with her but she told me, "There are always reasons for things."

Aunt Hildy died the following summer. She had bought herself another toad but because it wasn't Barnes, it didn't get any of the care that she gave her former pal. I think that toad died, but he may have just escaped when she wasn't paying attention. I asked her why the toad wasn't by his pond and she told me, "There are always reasons for things."

Several years later, I went to college to become a writer. My professors were all different in their personalities and styles and it impressed me how such different people could share the common passion of writing. The only belief they shared was that a writer should write about what he knows. All I knew about was waking up and going to school and wondering what everyone else was doing on Friday and Saturday nights. Nothing about my life was worth a story, nothing except Aunt Hildy and I couldn't figure her out.

Even so, Aunt Hildy became the subject of pretty much every assignment I did that first year. I would describe her house and her appearance and her cooking and weave in some story about what was behind her thinking or about her cross-country journey. I guess that I didn't do very well with my Aunt Hildy stories. I left school after seeing my second semester grades.

I bought a tan convertible and a toad named Bartholomew and, late one evening, got on the highway and simply headed east. I turned back for home when I realized that I was doing something pointless. Fortunately, my epiphany arrived only three hundred miles into the journey. I set Bartholomew free from his shoebox as I awaited breakfast at Denny's. The day after my brief trip, I got a job at a dry cleaners and I also managed to finagle my way into enrolling for the semester that was to begin the following week.

Nobody knows the reasons for my trip. Even I only have theories. My life has changed so much since then, I don't know what I was really thinking at the time. I used to think that I wanted to retrace Aunt Hildy's steps as if it were a quest of sorts. Perhaps I could reach some enlightenment by understanding her theories about beets and toads and Houston.

Lately, however, I think that people find themselves traveling in strange directions for unclear purposes because they react to something with a strangely placed first step. The rest of the steps are just consequences of the first one. I'm glad I turned around in time and came home.

The only thing I am sure about from my brief trip was that freeing the toad at Denny's was stupid, although it was fun to see the reaction it got. When the Denny's manager asked me if I knew how a toad got stuck in their cash register, I looked at him and responded, "There are always reasons for things."

His reaction surprised me. He simply nodded at the truth of my words.

The Gwen Tablets

After three days, Roscoe finally emerged from the cave. In each hand, he held a large tablet. He looked down to the bottom of the mountain and saw a few villagers suddenly sitting upright and shouting and shaking the other villagers until both an excited crowd and its loud cheer rose up to greet him.

Roscoe shook his head and despite his distance, they were suddenly quiet. Thirty minutes later, when he finally stood before the villagers, he explained.

"This is not about cheering," he said. "You should not cheer. You should never cheer. It distracts you from the message of the tablets. It distracts you from the rules we must now live by. Life has a purpose and unnecessary noise keeps you from that purpose."

Many in the crowd looked at what Roscoe called the Gwen Tablets but they couldn't see anything other than their consistent whiteness. There was nothing to read on the side they could see.

"Don't look at the tablets!" shouted Roscoe. "Look at your lives instead. See how easily you get distracted. I will tell you what you need to know. If I don't say something, you don't need to know it."

All 383 villagers stared at Roscoe, waiting for his next words. Nothing else mattered. He had been to the top of the mountain. He had entered the cave. He held the Gwen Tablets. The villagers waited for him to tell them all they needed to know to live their lives correctly.

"You have been waiting for me for three days," Roscoe said. "Many of you are very tired. What I have to share with you is too important to share with a tired audience. Lie down where you are and sleep. I will continue tomorrow."

The 383 villagers quietly got down on the ground. Most of them had been standing on cool and thick grass. They were quite comfortable lying where they were. Roscoe had also been standing on the thick grass so he too found a peaceful sleep.

There were maybe forty or so villagers, however, who had been standing on rocky dirt. They found no comfort lying where they had been standing. They found no sleep where they had been standing either. Within an hour, they were all sitting up, staring at Roscoe, and watching him sleep peacefully next to the Gwen Tablets.

The nonsleepers all seemed to slowly stand at the same time. Together they quietly stepped over those who slept on the thick grass. As if with one mind, they approached where Roscoe slept. They shared the same purpose, to see the other side of the Gwen Tablets, the side that Roscoe hadn't yet allowed them to see.

The nonsleepers who reached Roscoe and the Gwen Tablets first saw the blank side of the tablets. They waited for the other nonsleepers before making a move to turn the tablets over and see the secrets that had been hidden from them.

The Gwen Tablets were heavy and required several people to turn them over without making any noise. After those who were gathered by the tablets realized that the other side was also blank, they all quietly walked alone to places on the thick grass where they could sleep comfortably. And they all did.

Being so close to the Gwen Tablets had given the late sleepers wisdom without needing any chiseled words. They all realized that they needed Roscoe to lead them. They might not like all his rules, but they knew he offered them the best rules to live by and survive in the cold world that surrounded their village, mountain, and thick grass.

It didn't matter if he had any supernatural legitimacy or not. The villagers would all follow him. Those who saw the blank tablets would never tell anyone what they saw. They wouldn't even discuss it with each other. They would be loyal. They would follow whatever rules Roscoe shared with them. They would have faith.

As a result of Roscoe's leadership, the people of the village and their descendants were usually kept safe. The people of the village were also usually very happy, even in the middle of a difficult world.

And as she looked down at the village from her cloud-shaped home, Gwen was happy that she chose Roscoe to bring a message of hope to the villagers. Others would have asked her questions beginning with "what" or "why." Roscoe only cared about "how."

The Camden Blockbuster

The Camden Blockbuster was a memory from a faded pennant. She took his hand and they walked into a courtyard. "I could have been great," he told her, "pushed into a strange new life, but great!"

She consoled him with her generous eyes. He was a clown, but he was the only person she had ever met who knew all the steps. She hoped that he would remember all of them.

Out of her back pocket she pulled a well-worn page from a book long discarded. She opened her mouth and sang out the words on the page.

The Camden Blockbuster was unimpressed. He was asleep.

Wet Dogs of Hispaniola

Lundly, of "stepping in a puddle" fame, took the loudest book from the top shelf in the special "look scholarly or get out" section of the city library. The cracking it made, even though Lundly opened it slowly, gained him the suspicious attentions of Bea Lockabailly, the librarian with the meanest stare and consequently the highest rank in the library pecking order.

Lundly closed the book slowly and headed toward the only unoccupied table in the place. He could feel the heat of her stare as he walked on the eighty-seven-year-old floor. She could hear his shoes squeak as she wondered if he wasn't the one she had heard about with the puddles.

He pulled out the wooden chair and sat down to look at the book. Sure, there were a few books on the table to push aside, but he was up to the challenge.

"Hey, what's this?" thought Lundly about the biggest of the books on the table. "This looks like a book about embarrassing female problems and stuff like that. Maybe if I push it a little farther away..."

Bea Lockabailly was standing over Lundly shortly after the sound of a book landing squarely on the floor reverberated across the library. She stared at him and he leaned down, picked up the book, and handed it to her.

"*Embarrassing Female Problems and Stuff Like That*, by JeriLee Pinchfeathers," read Bea. "This is a very rare book, sir, almost as rare as its demand."

Lundly remained silent and considered his options. He had a book in front of him that he feared opening because it would probably once again crack. He knew that if he sat still and quiet, he would look suspicious. He could discuss the merits of the book Ms. Lockabailly was holding but that seemed like the best option to forget first. With no choices to tempt him, Lundly would wing it.

"Ms. Lockabailly, are the first recorded dewfalls too entwined in rural mythology to compare and contrast to those alluded to in Elizabethan sonnets?" he asked the still-staring Bea. "My friend and I have wagered some tacos."

It is the duty of all good librarians to find the answers to all questions presented by the curious members of the general public. With Pavlovian immediacy, Bea went off to find a reference book or two to find an answer for Lundly. Lundly opened the book and once again, it cracked.

The pages on the left side were all written in Spanish and the right side of the book had the English translation. Lundly looked up to see Bea Lockabailly peeking at him from between two tall stacks of books on her desk. She looked at him suspiciously.

He decided to read the pages that were opened in front of him. Unfortunately, the translation was made centuries before and required another level of translation to provide Lundly with some sort of clue to what the book was about. He turned the page.

His eyes fixed on the words "Wet Dogs of Hispaniola" and instead of looking at the succeeding words, his mind considered the possibilities of Wet Dogs of Hispaniola. Perhaps the Wet Dogs of Hispaniola could be the heroes or villains of a comic book, a novel, a movie, or maybe a line of toys. "Teenage Mutant Ninja Wet Dogs of Hispaniola," considered Lundly.

He looked up and there was Bea Lockabailly once again standing over him. She was holding two books.

"Maybe yes and maybe no," she said to him.

"I'm sorry, I was lost in a marketing campaign," apologized Lundly. "What did you say?"

Bea took the chair across the table and repeated her words to Lundly. He still looked puzzled.

"This blue book says yes and this orange book says no," she explained. "Which way will get you the tacos? I'll even Xerox it for you if you find it worthwhile to share your winnings with me."

Lundly considered his current options. He could admit that there was really no taco wager. He could take Bea Lockabailly for tacos. He could even close and open the book and maybe the sound of the book opening would get him thrown out of the library before he had to face one of the other options. Yes, this choice was good and would do nicely.

The book, however, made no noise as Lundly opened it to the title page. He looked down to see that it was the diary of one of Christopher Columbus' captains. In that context, he reconsidered the possibilities of the "Wet Dogs of Hispaniola." Bea stared at him, refusing to give up on a chance for free tacos. She went and made copies of pages from both books and returned to startle him out of his revised marketing campaign.

"Look, here are two different arguments with different results about the influence of dewfall mythology," said Bea. "I have written my name and number on the top of this one. If you feel that you should share your winnings with me, give me a call."

Lundly looked up at her and asked her to sit down.

"What do you know about the Wet Dogs of Hispaniola?" he asked. "And how would you market them?"

"A lot and T-shirts," Bea replied. "My father was a professor of Caribbean history at the University of Someplace Exclusive and I read every book he used for his classes. T-shirts are definitely the way to go. Functional and cultural, they provide a canvas for those who have something to say, sell, or draw."

There was a long pause as Lundly stared at the wall behind Bea. He snapped back to reality and broke the silence.

"Did you want to go for tacos now?" he asked, and she nodded.

They left and discussed the deeper meanings behind their earlier shallow conversations. Lundly, however, was on autopilot as they sat at an outdoor table in front of the taco stand. While Bea spoke, he skillfully nodded and said things like "oh, wow," at the right times while he concentrated on pondering the possibilities of the day.

Bea could help him market the Wet Dogs of Hispaniola and turn the concept into money. She could tell him the facts about them and turn the Wet Dogs into understanding. She could even tell him why she blushed years ago when she first read the words "Wet Dogs of Hispaniola" in her father's textbook, and there could be some fun involved.

Lundly looked down at his shoes and wondered when he had walked into another puddle. The opportunities Bea presented would have to wait to be considered until he was alone in bed that night. Fortunately, that night he gained an insight into the deeper meanings of life as he thought about all that Bea offered and how his wet socks distracted him as she spoke.

And If Not for the Sky, We Shall Have Planets at Our Doorsteps

Queenie should have stuck to her shopping that rainy evening, but the man seemed so convincing that she hung on his every syllable. He stood on a mall bench and spoke to several people, mainly men who waited for their wives to finish shopping.

He rambled on but was gifted at the task. Queenie stared at his lips as she followed his words.

"Man does not deserve the Earth, and the animals that seem so placid all know this, they do," he said. "They shall one day try to take the planet away as once they had the world to themselves before. The sun was shining and there were no manmade waves across the sky. Man does not deserve the sky and once the animals fail at their initial task and man is still in the world – because man has shoes that keep the dirt down and man has nails that can keep the Earth itself secured under boards and walkways – the animals shall then look up to the sky and conspire with the birds to carry the sky away, perhaps to Venus, although Neptune is a strong possibility. Man cannot nail down the sky."

The speaker left his lofty bench and grabbed a bag from a man in a red flannel shirt. Reaching into the bag he pulled out a package of nails. Returning to stand on the bench, he opened the package and flung a handful of nails into the air to punctuate his next words.

"Man's nails are of no use to him to keep the sky so dear so close. Without sky, there will be no beauty, nothing to keep the clouds and planets up. And if not for sky we shall have planets at our doorsteps. We will have to leave through back doors forever. Relations driving in from points north shall simply pass us by and not be able to see our addresses, which now shine so clearly that happy drivers in passing cars can now look and say, 'See there, that is house number 863, and there on my side, look, there is number 858.' I have seen the future and it is quite inconvenient."

A security guard and several others were gathered around the speaker by this time, but Queenie didn't notice them at all. She awaited the speaker's next words. The security guard also seemed intrigued.

"My friends, the time is now so check your watches. To those of you who do not heed my words, you shall have sorrow and find yourselves without visitors, without people to show off how your family room looks with new paneling. You shall regret not being among the fortunate few who secured private post office boxes far from the falling planets. Take heed for it is not too late, follow my message."

As the man left, Queenie was the only one following. He walked into a nearby diner and sat at the counter. Queenie took a nearby booth and stared at him as she ordered three dollars worth of food to secure her table.

The man ordered a burger and fries and some iced tea. He followed up the meal with an unrecognizable dessert. He paid his check and left.

Queenie ran after him, but a strong waitress detained her until she paid for her uneaten order. The time she spent paying the check caused her to almost lose the man. She only caught a glimpse of him as he turned into an alley. When she reached the alley, he was nowhere to be seen.

Queenie walked slowly in the rain as she thought about how to find the man who had so enthralled her. Who was he? Where did he go? What was the dessert he ate?

She found herself in front of a private postal center and decided to go inside. She bought the biggest-sized box they had despite the fact that the price was five times the going rate. Queenie didn't care about the money. She would be prepared when the sky was gone and a planet fell on her doorstep. No letters or catalogs would miss her now. She whistled happily as she walked home, not turning to see that the man who had spoken so convincingly at the mall entered the postal center immediately after she left.

He was paid on commission.

The Sawdust Rabbits

There were two kinds of sawdust rabbits residing in the local collection of murky caves. One kind was made of a much finer grain, although it was suspected that the wood used was of a much poorer quality than that used in the coarser grain of the other rabbits. Whatever the case, there were two kinds of sawdust rabbits.

Now there was talk that perhaps the two kinds of sawdust rabbits should not associate with each other. There was also talk that maybe things would be better if the two kinds of rabbits were forced to mingle with each other at an early age. Around the local collection of murky caves, there was a lot of talk.

An older rabbit who was very knowledgeable in the political systems in other groups of caves decided that the matter should be put to a vote. The rabbits agreed, as they wanted to decide once and for all what was the right way for them to live. They sought an answer, so they agreed to put the question to a vote.

There was much commotion around the caves as the more vocal of the sawdust rabbits shouted that rabbits must vote their way. The more subdued rabbits listened intently.

The decision was finally made on the relationship between the two kinds of sawdust rabbits. The rabbits were excited. They had just decided what was right and what was wrong by voting. They wanted to do it again. So they voted again. There was more and more commotion around the caves. And they voted again and again.

The rabbits voted on every truth they could think of. They decided that the sun revolved around the Earth, that tomatoes were blue, and that Kanye West was incredibly talented. Somebody suggested that the sawdust rabbits vote on whether or not there was a God. So they voted. And they voted no.

The next day, there was a fire that burned up the entire population of sawdust rabbits. The foxes in the area believe that a rabbit rabbi who was disenchanted with the vote started the fire. Others look up into the sky with fear and reverence when they talk about the fire. But there are a few who don't really pay much attention to either opinion because they know that whatever is the truth is the truth – and no amount of opinion one way or the other can change it.

And it really doesn't matter whether you agree with that or not.

Days of Cloud Claiming

There were too many bills in the stack on the table for Wallace to think clearly about anything without panicking. He was rapidly losing ground financially so he chose instead to think about his relationships with women. Alas, he found himself subscribing to the belief that all women were crazy, a theory initially proposed by his cousin. In other words, he wasn't currently in a relationship and had no real prospects to change that.

Wallace needed to find an arena in his life in which he could claim some success. He needed desperately to impose himself on some aspect of his environment. He took a drive until he was too bothered by the noises his car made to think clearly. When he was safely back home, he tried to type out a list of possibilities into his computer but the screen went black.

Wallace decided to take a hot shower and sing some of his favorite operas. Before he could realize that he knew no opera songs (beyond repeating "Figaro"), the hot water ran out. The water heater had gone on the fritz yet again.

Still lost in his troubles, Wallace went for a walk and happened to look up. There they were. The answer to his problems was right above him. He saw a cloud and decided to claim it as his own. He yelled out at the top of his lungs, "That cloud is mine! The cloud that looks like a couple of otters is mine!"

A few people looked at him but nobody contradicted him. As far as they were concerned, if he wanted the cloud, he could have it. With nobody to offer any opposition, Wallace claimed another cloud. "The one that looks like a seamstress with a harmonica is mine also!" he shouted. Again, nobody offered any opposition.

Wallace soon had a problem, however, as he noticed the gentle breezes of springtime pushing his two clouds slowly eastward. He looked at the new batch of clouds that approached from the west, but none of them were worth shouting about. He decided instead to follow the two clouds and let more people know that those clouds were his.

Wallace ran down the street telling everybody in his path that the otter cloud and the seamstress with the harmonica cloud were both his. His and his alone. Nobody offered any opposition. Nobody rebutted his claim. In fact, people seemed to give him more room to continue his eastward trek. People gave him plenty of room.

He was excited. When he returned home for some root beer, he looked forward to doing the same thing the next day. He set his alarm for dawn and he was back outside by 6:15 that morning.

The first cloud worth Wallace's claim appeared on the western horizon at about 10:30 a.m. "That cloud, the one that looks like a Buick hubcap besieged by iguanas, is mine, all mine!" he shouted. Again, there was no opposition. That wasn't good enough for Wallace, however. This lack of opposition was due to the lack of other people. Wallace needed to make his claim in front of other people in order for it to mean anything.

He ran into the donkey shop a block east of his apartment. There were four people inside, as well as several donkeys and a burro. "There is a cloud that looks like a Buick hubcap besieged by iguanas overhead and it's mine, all mine," Wallace explained to the group of strangers. "That is all."

He ran back outside and made the same report to all of the businesses on the block. Unfortunately, when he continued his activities on the next block, he ran into a police station and was promptly restrained by two officers who took him to the front counter.

"You're the same one who did this yesterday?" asked the woman behind the counter. Wallace promptly agreed, proud of the field of cloud claiming he was pioneering. She told him he was under arrest.

He was told that he had broken the law the day before when he ran down the street cloud claiming. It seems that he made the transition between taking a shower and running around outside too quickly and without all of the steps necessary to avoid the town's indecency laws.

Things were not all bad for Wallace, however. His social life picked up as he began dating the policewoman who worked behind the counter. To Wallace, women were no longer all crazy. To the policewoman, however, Wallace was as loony as could be imagined, but she liked the idea of shouting out her claim to his dimpled buns.

The Bucket Seats of Poets

We're the eighty to your hundred. We're the crisper to your luncheon, and we plowed the sacred stanzas far beneath the copper clouds. We're the Mormons in your wallet, the high tooth of your umbrella and we walk around the plaza like a plant unfurling seals.

We're the toast in your iguana, the parfait that clogs your sauna. You're abreast of all we offer if you choose to read the tonic. We'll be French before you know it. Not a chance that we'd be rhymers, for our shadows never fall twice on a shifting grain of rice.

Call us any cab you think of. We're the bucket seats of poets. We're the ample chants around a crispy fire.

We're now sixty to your carpet and we didn't speak of talc yet. We have a busy plane before us so we really should resign. Tell your body twin we meant well, and forgive us for the round sell. We're the fever in the freezer and like smoke, we must take heart.

Methods of Obtaining Pizza

We often call for a pizza delivery. Maybe even weekly.

Other times, we'll stop by a pizza place, usually the one around the corner. Actually, it's only one of us who will have that task. Either she or I will stop on the way home. If she buys the pizza, she orders a Diet Coke.

Rarely do we ever buy frozen pizzas but we are both aware of that possibility and maybe every other year, we will have a frozen pizza in our freezer as an extra option.

Lance's Toboggan of Miracles

Zenith heard her Jeep's left rear tire explode and she knew it wouldn't be long before the rhinos would overtake her. Her life flashed before her. She remembered her parents telling her not to go. She pictured her girlfriends begging her not to go. She thought about Meldwich the butcher telling her to change perfumes.

Now this.

She heard the approaching rhinos and wondered how to spend her last moments on Earth. Suddenly, she heard a "Ho, ho, ho." She knew that could only mean one thing. She looked up and there it was – Lance's Toboggan of Miracles.

"Climb aboard and hurry," said Lance who was standing in the spectacular toboggan. He was holding its steering wheel in one hand and releasing the rope ladder with the other. "No time to lose, Zenith," he said. "We are needed elsewhere."

In Midway City, Hector looked over the reports placed on his desk by the grinning police detective. There would be no avoiding the consequences now. He was going to jail. Even after turning over so many of his friends to the police to avoid this fate over the years, he was going to jail. He feared what awaited him there, surrounded by so many angry ex-friends.

"Isn't there something you could do?" Hector inquired as he took off his Rolex and placed it in front of he detective. The detective picked up the watch and studied it before placing it into his pocket.

"No," was all he said.

"Ho, ho, ho," was all Lance said as he stopped the Toboggan of Miracles outside the window of the fifteenth floor office. Lance carefully cut a large square in the window as the policeman smiled and waved. Hector climbed out into the toboggan and they were off. The policeman stuck his head and shoulders through the hole in the window, still waving.

"Hector this is Zenith, Zenith this is Hector," said Lance. "It's time for burgers."

The Toboggan of Miracles touched down in front of an In-N-Out and they all went inside to order. This one was more than a simple drive-through. No one said much and whatever may have been said wasn't responded to. Soon they were back in the sky.

They flew around for a while. They stopped for more burgers and flew around again. Hours became days. Days became weeks. Flying, stopping for burgers, flying, stopping for burgers, flying, stopping for burgers. At about the same time, both Zenith and Hector cracked.

"We can't take this anymore!" they shouted in unison as if they had that moment well-rehearsed. "Please take us back where you found us!"

Hector's office was the closest, so Lance's Toboggan of Miracles headed there first. Hector got out and climbed back through the same window he had used for his escape. He promised to write even though he never would.

Inside he found the same police detective sitting in his office waiting for him. Sitting in the chairs on each side of him were the detective's children.

"They want to hear all about Lance and his Toboggan of Miracles," he said.

Hector told them all about the flying and the stops for burgers as the children and the detective sat transfixed.

"You know, Hector, you may be a crook but you're really not a bad sort of guy," said the detective when it was clear that Hector's story had adequately covered both aspects of the journey. "How about if you turn in somebody you know for another crime and I'll pretend like I never saw these reports."

Hector pulled out a photograph of his brother Wally leaving a gas station while waving the large block of wood attached to the bathroom key. Wally was thrown into prison. Hector lived happily ever after on the money he had embezzled.

The Toboggan of Miracles soon descended next to where Zenith's Jeep had blown out a tire. The Jeep was nowhere to be seen. In its place, however, was a brand new Pontiac Firebird that had recently been stolen. Some car thieves had decided to trade it for the Jeep. They figured that the Jeep owner was probably trampled to death in the rhino stampede and if they stayed in the bright red Firebird, they would be arrested for sure.

Zenith got into the Firebird, claiming it as her own and Lance tossed pieces of cardboard off of the Toboggan of Miracles. Each landed perfectly over a different window of the car. The toboggan hovered over the Firebird as Lance poured bright blue paint over the car. When all the red had been covered, Lance's Toboggan of Miracles flew away. The wind created by the toboggan's departure swirled around the now-blue car, blowing off the cardboard, and drying the paint.

Zenith drove across three continents until she was back home. She changed her perfume and married Meldwich the butcher.

At this very moment, Lance is out flying somewhere in his Toboggan of Miracles. Then again, he may have stopped for burgers.

Slapped the Bellman Not Once

When the ballroom dancer sails her past to Spain, she will still be the blue one in the scenery. Some friends would ask. I knew better. The sky was out. The dense were strong. You ought to be in pictures.

Edgar stood in the minnow's crater. Just the way you thought about stains. Freda wrote something in her blue nook. My keys are missing. Onions ruled. Laughter prevents vibrations. Deeper than you can imagine is an otter in a jumpsuit. Give it time and you will be someone's equator.

She slapped the bellman not once, but more times. Unless you squeeze, you will miss out on the most needed portions of the family scrapbook. Has the carp really gone? And my keys with him? Seas of misunderstandings prevent the blue envelopes from rusting on the canopy. Your balcony sucks. Tall people eat some red things.

A policeman asked about his name. The bell didn't ring, but some pelicans shuddered. Onions have fallen out of favor. It was in print. Many things moved one way or became whiskers. Lost my keys or I would stop. Horses patterned after Yolanda's desktop. Forget the onions. Cast them out. Cast them all out. Found my keys. Bye.

He Shares All His Envelopes & Is Beloved

1. Everything feels slumber. Friends are still but the clock progresses. A burning engine floods the deepest feelings of Oscar who plans new ways of shining shoes. His stand has been too quiet of late.

2. Dexter stands by an orange pilot. The nearby bank is empty. His bag of popcorn is plain. He uses no salt... no sodium at all. Somewhere it feels like autumn.

3. The day behind was the day ahead. The day beyond that too has been played. Only Saturday has promise.

4. Someone in suspenders surveys his contented office. The workers look up in smileless admiration. He shares all his envelopes and is beloved. His purple hat is not a factor. All his quirks are forgiven.

5. Marie counts digits. Stan surveys her legs and estimates their softness. Oscar waits outside by his stand. The new sign has attracted the curious.

6. Dexter now stands beside a green tailgunner. He talks of promises broken and fields of salamander. His day is never complete without broccoli beside his main course. The curtains are now open but the weather seems unconcerned.

7. Recycled emotions descend upon the reheated coffee patrons. A final doughnut calls out to Sullivan. He stares but he has his hands full of new envelopes. He is happy to work where he does.

8. Estelle pictures her desk covered with glitter. She polishes the glass that protects the photograph of the one she shared passion with long enough to commit to. Tomorrow is his birthday. She may shop on Saturday.

9. Once dreaming was possible. Now is a time when all joys are simple. New envelopes. Shoeshines on the cutting edge of creativity. Air force veterans in different rainbow shades. Where have all the money dreams gone and what preceded them?

10. Carrying a flask is Bernard. "Such an ox," think the others. He wonders whether to order the velvet portrait or become a Republican.

11. Things change but time holds prisoners.

Bragging Alfred

Alfred liked being an American but since he never left the country he had nobody to brag about being an American to. Everyone he ever met was an American.

"I have nobody to brag to," he thought to himself.

Alfred moved to Finland where he has no friends.

Billboard Thor

Thor wanted to be a billboard. He would stand along a state highway all day with his arms outstretched and tell people in passing cars to buy vodka. He dreamed of wearing lights so people could see him at night.

One day, he managed to get a vodka company to buy him lights. He was wearing five hundred pounds worth of lighting when a strong wind blew him over. He is probably still out on the highway, lying flat on his back.

Pondering Attila (The Scooting Eagle)

Audrey sat at one of the outdoor plastic tables near the university's King Hall as she read the history book that was open before her. She looked up and gazed at a fruit tree across the campus as she pondered Attila's motives and strategies. On the concrete between the tables, an eagle scooted by.

Suddenly, Audrey looked down at the eagle. The eagle stopped and stared up at her.

"You scooted!" Audrey said. "I have never known an eagle to scoot."

The eagle looked up at her as if she had discovered some terrible secret about him. He was a clever eagle, however, and he decided to try to distract her from her discovery about his ability to scoot. He hopped up on the table and they exchanged introductions. All the while, the eagle was planning his next move.

"You're pondering Attila's motives and strategies," he said. "I have never known an Audrey to ponder Attilla."

There was a long pause as both Audrey and the eagle reached an apparent stalemate. She seemed a bit nervous and the eagle decided that he had indeed snatched a tie from the jaws of defeat.

"You're a better debater than most of the birds that come around here," conceded Audrey.

"Thank you," replied the eagle. "Well, it's been nice chatting with you, Audrey, but I am afraid I must scoot."

The eagle scooted away proudly. He had been successful in avoiding a potential catastrophe. He had almost revealed the truth that all eagles have the ability to scoot, perhaps tipping the balance of nature against his entire species.

When he was miles away, high in flight and searching for his dinner, he chuckled. He was a clever eagle and he knew it. He had talked his way out of a dangerous situation.

Meanwhile, back at the outdoor table at the university, similar thoughts were going through the head of Audrey the mouse.

A Call from Wally (6:14 a.m.)

Wally called from the pay phone at the liquor store. "It's about time for another package," he told me. "This time, *you* get out the ribbons and masking tape."

I looked at the clock and had trouble focusing enough to decipher the time. I asked Wally. After learning that it was fourteen minutes after six, my curiosity grew enough for me to finally ask with whom I was speaking.

"It's me, Wally and I'm at the liquor store telephone."

"I don't know any Wally."

"Yes, you do. You know Wally Cleaver, Wally Gator, that guy with the annoying laugh who hangs around with David and Ricky Nelson, and me. I was the one wearing the Mr. Bill shirt."

"What Mr. Bill shirt?" I asked, hoping that the style or color would help jar my memory.

"The blue one. You remember me. About six years ago we rode an elevator up to the sixth floor at the American Flag Bank Building. Well, actually I got off on the fifth floor."

"What did we talk about on the ride?"

"Well, actually nothing. We were riding up with this woman in a bright red dress. Low cut. We smiled at each other briefly when we noticed that we were each surveying her dress."

"Her I remember."

"Well, since then I found out where she works and I've been sending her gifts and signing it 'The Two Guys from the Elevator.' So get out your ribbons and masking tape. I've bought her another gift."

"You're crazy."

"That may well be but I have bought her a beautiful color television. Will you help me wrap it?"

"No just send it to her as is," I replied.

He decided to do just that and hung up the phone. I tried to get some sleep but the woman I live with had heard the strange call and seemed suspicious and when she was concerned, it bothered me too.

"Well, you and I share a wonderful life together," I started to explain. "Our life is filled with many beautiful things that we truly enjoy. Wally will be sending us a television next."

Floyd Marveled at Walter's Couches

Walter was a couch designer in Boston. As it happened, he was the worst couch designer in all of New England. People would come from miles around to marvel at the poor quality of his work. One such visitor was Floyd from Buffalo, an expert pencil painter.

Floyd was voted "Top Pencil Painter in New York State" six out of the previous seven years. When Floyd went to Boston to see the terrible couches designed by Walter, the two men met. They compared their work.

Walter was impressed by the work of Floyd. Floyd, however, spent an enjoyable afternoon laughing at the work of Walter. When Floyd returned to Buffalo, he was shot by a sniper. Walter is still designing terrible couches.

Lena in Other Lifetimes

Lena could have been louder in another lifetime if she thought hard enough. She could have been more determined, more daring, or perhaps more conservative.

But not Lena. She was in touch with herself in other lifetimes and was well aware of what she could do if she put her mind to it. A little research at the library and she could pass along the information necessary for any of the previous Lenas to be heralded as a mystic.

That wouldn't do, however.

She could have asked the right questions of future Lenas and she could be the mystic. She could be a lottery winner or a stock market wizard. But not Lena. That just wouldn't do.

She could be the inventor of something amazing, just by talking to the Lenas of the future and finding something she could reproduce before the scheduled inventor fulfilled his potential.

Nope. Not this option either for Lena.

Lena could have whatever she wanted from the richest of all the Lenas, Duchess Lena who lived in a castle in the seventeenth century. Duchess Lena would be more than willing to bury a treasure that she could enjoy in a later lifetime. One look out her castle window at the alternative, living as one of the common masses, would scare the duchess into leaving the best of her belongings in a buried box.

This would do nicely, thought Lena.

It was a hot May day when Lena started her long journey to a village on a small island. She spent the time on the airplane deep in concentration, contacting Duchess Lena who told her about the gold and jewels in the box she would bury in the side of the third-tallest hill surrounding the village. Meanwhile, Lena's husband, Fred, sat quietly beside her and pretended to find something of interest in the airline's magazine.

A small boat got them to the island and a rented car took them to the site. Fred dug and found the box as Lena and Duchess Lena gossiped across the centuries. Fred stepped aside and Lena opened the box. Inside was everything she expected. Fred, who hadn't seriously expected to find anything, was in awe.

Before he had time to adjust to the newly found wealth, however, Lena grabbed a bracelet and pointed to the newly dug hole. She told Fred to bury the box back in it. He was less than enthusiastic about parting with the box that he had traveled halfway around the world to find, but he figured that there was some reason for Lena's request. It wasn't until the two were back on an airplane heading home that Lena stopped talking to the Lenas from other lifetimes long enough to explain it all to him.

As much as Lena would have enjoyed what the treasure could have given her in her current lifetime, a future Lena needed it more. This future Lena would be giving up a large inheritance to marry a poor man, someone whom her parents would hate enough to disown her. Just as Fred started to complain that he shouldn't have to do without the treasure just because a future Lena would marry some loser, the current Lena stopped him.

"He is a future Fred," she explained, and the current Fred was quiet for the rest of the flight.

Model Minerva

Model Minerva shuffled over to where the handicapped ramp could accommodate her. A healthy woman, she had more of a struggle than she should with the ankle-hemmed skirt that restricted her steps.

"Somebody is supposed to buy this?" she asked a member of the fashion show staff. He looked at her silently, not being paid to answer.

"The black evening gown is by somebody French and may be worn with pearls or a simple pendant, or even a full set of Cherokee feathers, for that matter," said the polished voice into the microphone as Model Minerva shuffled along the lit runway in the midst of the people sitting in darkness.

She reached the end of the runway, turned almost gracefully, and fell down into the arms of someone she couldn't see.

It was a man, decided Model Minerva, since she was lifted so easily back onto the runway. His touch was warm and she felt emotions she had never known before. She faced away from him as he lifted her and he was seated back in the darkness before she could catch an adequate glimpse.

Model Minerva shuffled carefully back along the runway to the side of the curtains from which she had emerged earlier. She quickly changed into the blouse and skirt she had worn from home and went to join the audience. She hoped there was an empty chair where she could wait until the show was over and the lights were turned on. She decided that she was in love and she was anxious to see who she was in love with.

Her goal of finding a chair was successful. She concentrated her efforts on trying to determine which of the dark silhouettes against the lit runway was the man she loved. There were two possibilities. One was a tall man with short hair. The other was a shorter man with broad shoulders.

"This is insane!" Model Minerva thought loudly to herself. "My heart is beating quickly from the touch of a man I never saw. I am looking for the man I think I love and I have no idea what he looks like."

The man with the broad shoulders stood up and left the room before Model Minerva could respond. The show was about to end and she believed her chances were better to meet the taller one than to try to chase the one who had left.

"I appreciate your thanks, but I wasn't the one who caught you," said the taller man to a very disappointed Minerva. "He left early to catch a plane."

Model Minerva stood silently while the tall man asked if he could buy her a drink. He suggested a place he knew and they left together.

His name was Henry and he was the owner of a large department store chain. She was impressed, although her thoughts were on the other man. Henry, however, was rich, good-looking and intelligent. She considered his offer of a weekend on his yacht.

Henry wasn't the one she had wanted, but he looked strong enough that he could have caught her if she had stumbled a few feet further down the runway. She rationalized herself into a yes. The weekend was great fun although Model Minerva still thought about the other man's touch.

"Minerva, I would like to see you again," he said as he drove her to her apartment. She smiled and looked into his eyes, hoping to find a reason to forget the other man's touch.

"A friend of mine is opening up his new nightclub next weekend," Minerva said. "I would really like you to be my guest."

"I can't, Minerva, my wife has made other plans for us," he said. She looked startled.

"I'm sorry, I thought you knew," he said. "Here is an envelope with something to make you forget any trouble I may have caused you."

Model Minerva was too startled to return the envelope. She said nothing to the man as she got out of his car. She was in tears before she reached her door.

She telephoned the modeling agency and notified them she was quitting as a model. "I was happier working in my father's restaurant as a waitress," she explained.

A year or so later, Waitress Minerva was taking the dinner orders from a well-dressed couple in her father's restaurant. The man kept staring at her, which made her uneasy.

"If he wasn't so good-looking, I'd tell him off," thought Waitress Minerva.

Later, she served him coffee and he became bolder in his staring.

"Do you have a problem?" she asked him coldly.

"I apologize, but you look familiar," he said politely. "Perhaps I met you at a party?"

"That's an old line," she responded.

"Still, I can't keep from picturing you wearing a black evening gown and... stumbling! I remember now, you were the model I caught when you fell off the stage!" he said.

Waitress Minerva's heart beat rapidly. Here was the man with the wonderful touch, and he was more handsome than he had to be to have her heart. She was too embarrassed about how they had met to admit he was right about who she was.

"Your company should be returning soon," Waitress Minerva reminded him.

"No," he said. "She is out of my life for good. We broke up tonight."

He invited her for a drink when she was through with work for the night and after explaining things to her father, she was immediately through with work for the night.

The man, whose name was Ronald, spoke as Waitress Minerva stared into his eyes and followed every word.

"He is perfect," she thought to herself. "Kind, intelligent, a dream."

One thought, however, troubled her about this apparently sensitive man. How could he have broken up with someone and be so sure that things were over? A few minutes later, Ronald explained his reasons.

"I have one problem with women," he said. "I am possessive. Very possessive. Now, don't get me wrong. I would enjoy every success that the woman in my life has. And I don't have fits of jealousy. I wouldn't follow a woman around or question her about what she did if she was late coming home.

"The woman I was with was my fiancée until tonight," he continued. "I found out that she had slept with a friend of mine. She is a faithful woman, however. She just happened to have been intimate with a friend of mine before we met. I can't bear the thought of being married to someone who was intimate with a friend of mine. I won't have a wife whom any of my close friends have slept with. Tonight, I found out what happened seven years ago."

Waitress Minerva nodded and forced a smile. Ronald invited her on a romantic weekend and her smile was genuine.

"It will be wonderful," he said while he gazed into her eyes. "My brother, Henry, has a yacht and I'm sure he will let us use it."

Lido Branches (The Beginning)

From the tan cafe to her pink terrace, the intros were made and the tension threshold tightened. G-Man took Tulip to a grandstand of personal cheers. She leaned forward and tested his elbows. "Strong. Strong, indeed," she thought as she compared them to the version in her dreams.

Fresh from a stale bout with nothing more than idle suds, no matter how vicious, he was the waiter in the blue helicopter in her reruns of lofty illusions. The daylight drove to a halt upon the sudden piano of pleasure and they stood on flat wood and were grateful for the Italian fiasco that somber summer they would never be totally free of. They were one or two, but each played several roles. The evening drifted downward and G-Man wiped his Malaysian shoes clean of its vanishing embers. This was paradise in all of its welded together spots, like the nuts and bolts you see beyond the smiling machinery of a Disneyland ride.

Shift the scene quickly deep into night. Tulip lingers at the walrus rack wishing her favorite one for show had cleaner tusks. Alas, this was to be but the mere Buick of favorite nights. This was the first and raw it was. Yes siree. She stood in the doorway with a penguin instead. "This, my love is what I bring you," she told him with her eyes and possibly a rib or spleen also, "me in but a fragile slip of cloth and a penguin named Bartholomew."

He smiled and consulted the television schedule. Tossing it aside in a heap resembling the worst days of the French Empire, he took her hand and brought her to him. "These are for you," he said to her as she wondered where the penguin had run off to. She looked in his hand and there was some change, maybe a paperclip, a parking stub and matches from the Lido, and a couple of twigs.

There wasn't a great deal left to say and they managed to keep wordless and yet wake the neighbors. Tulip studied the pieces of twig on the Lido matchbook and wondered aloud if they were Lido branches. G-Man didn't leave, but the penguin had to get some air.

Rabid at Best (Episode II)

She was rabid at best as she whitewashed a meadow and passed out a tray to the wolf in the plow. The day had sharp edges that kept out the choices of what still remained of the bounce of a heart.

The lion had ventured below the equator and happier there, sent his squid and regrets. The shine-happy leopard was cast in her drama of rich parking meters and how they went bad. The long-distant usher stood closer than cobwebs behind a tall bush while awaiting a queue. She thought of her Hoover and dancing Decembers. Her sad silhouette mimed a target or two. The porcelain polish, her hair in a rainbow, she counted the words as if breaking his code. She couldn't conceive that a hand through the cobwebs would bring back bouquets and a romp in the hedges.

"Dear leopard," she said to the south-staring feline. "Dear leopard," she said with a purr and a growl. "The mountain became us before we could cross it. The months have since caved to a shadow and scowl.

"I think that the stage is the wrong place for talking. I think that the sky is too heavy in blue. I think that the hedges are holding the deuces and planned parade permits may soon be approved."

The usher beheld her in round conversation. Her stare was the one, but the road was now two. Transfixed like an eagle on the pawsteps of dinner, he stood like a Plymouth as she thought about turning.

Meely's Rules

Rule #1: Never bargain with a minister. Even if you win you lose.

Rule #2: Never sing more than one verse if you don't know the chorus.

Rule #3: Always park near a nicer vehicle than yours. If a car is stolen, it probably won't be yours.

Rule #4: Be serene when dealing with someone cooking oysters. Don't let your anger counteract the possible effects of the meal.

Rule #5: Be in gear whenever plausible.

Rule #6: If you have to stretch too many muscles, reconsider your goals.

Rule #7: Send cash to Meely. The bigger denominations are better.

Rule #8: Change lettuce types with the seasons. Romaine, butterhead, leaf, and iceberg offer a nice rotation when used in that order.

Rule #9: Send checks to Meely. Include lots of zeroes.

Rule #10: Be a friend to the person who dresses the best, but don't stand next to this individual at a party.

Rule #11:Walking is good for the pavement. It gives it purpose.

Rule #12:Never use the same vitamin more than once in the same sentence.

Rule #13:None of you have sent him any money yet. What gives?

Rule #14:Dogs are monosyllabic.

Revenge of the Breakfast

Buchanan walked over to the car that slowly rolled down the pathway onto his breakfast. "Damn," he thought. He reached into the open window and unlocked the car door, beginning the series of tasks required to stop the car. Buchanan's neighbor was designing linoleum somewhere in a back room and didn't hear the commotion that his car had caused.

Buchanan rang his neighbor's doorbell, preparing himself to demand three new eggs to replace the ones now embedded in his neighbor's tires. When, instead of his neighbor George, a floating genie named Sheila answered the door, Buchanan was startled. He babbled his rehearsed lines about how he should be given three eggs to replace the ones victimized by the rolling car. The genie misunderstood his request and turned him into someone who forgets faces.

Buchanan was reclining in his easy chair a couple of hours later when he realized his face was missing. "Now where did I leave it?" he said to himself. "Hey, I just can't remember!"

Excited by the new challenge that the day offered, he ran next door to ask his neighbor for some paper to keep a record of his search. Instead of his neighbor answering the door, however, a plastic surgeon said, "Hello," when Buchanan rang the bell. Recognizing the concern that was on the blank space in front of Buchanan's head, the plastic surgeon insisted on helping solve Buchanan's problem.

"You look like you could use some scrambled eggs," said the plastic surgeon. Breakfast was delicious and a good way to start a long search. Buchanan looked high and low for his face. He traveled by ship across the seven seas. He traveled by train and by bus. His efforts, however, were unfruitful.

"I'd face it if I could," he thought.

His neighbor eventually found the face. After sixty days of not hearing from Buchanan, George kept the second face. Buchanan went to Las Vegas where he is just another faceless lounge singer. George used his two faces in a highly successful political career.

When Fred Stood, the Band Played

Unbeknownst to most of the crowd, Fred was quietly ushered to a seat on the stage where the large cymbal player had been sitting reading *Esquire*. Fred took the cymbal player's seat and the one whose responsibility it was to start the proceedings fulfilled the trust he was given.

Henrietta looked up from her sheet music to see what was distracting the crowd. On the far side of the stage was her old boyfriend Fred. All the memories started coming back to her: the walks in the park, the incident with the lion tamer, the wax in the closet.

"Why is he here?" she wondered. "And why is he wearing a tie?"

Fred was introduced by name only. No title or reason for his apparent special treatment was explained over the public address system. He stood up and the bandleader gave the signal for the music to start. And start it did, although Henrietta was a bit off on her trombone playing.

"Why are we playing for Fred?" Henrietta wondered. "We have the mayor, the governor, civic leaders, and our hometown sports hero, and we are acknowledging Fred. Why is this?"

Henrietta again recalled Fred as someone who was good company on a walk, familiar with how to have fun with a lion tamer, and rather sloppy with wax. These three traits, however, were the only descriptions she could provide herself about Fred's fredness. For years, even he acknowledged that these were his sole unique traits, going so far as to list them at the top of his résumé.

"How did he get to be the center of attention here today?" she again wondered.

Somebody had shouted out an "atta boy!" in Fred's direction, and he stood up to wave back at the admirer. When he stood, the band again began to play. Henrietta played more correct notes this time, but she was still dazed by the happenings.

"Let me run things through my mind again," she thought before giving herself prompt permission. "Fred and I met at the park and continued to walk around there every other afternoon until the incident with the hedgehog. He was great company, but not as much fun as Fred.

"Fred looked through the yellow pages to find a way to make my birthday special. He found the lion tamer. Wow! Was that great or what? Then the wax. I still have to scrape it off the walls and floor of my closet. Perhaps with Formula 409?"

While Henrietta's mind considered appropriate cleansers, Fred stood up to wave at his second grade teacher who looked the same as she had three decades earlier, give or take thirty years. Right on cue, the band began to play.

This time, Henrietta was right in tune with her fellow musicians. She had gotten used to the idea that Fred was something special, even if she didn't know why. A few more times that afternoon, Fred stood up and each time, the band played. Henrietta played with increasing enthusiasm and accuracy. She was happy for Fred, for whatever reason she should be.

Henrietta was happier than she had been since her cosmetic surgery went awry. Her earlobes had been reduced to her satisfaction but as a result of the anesthetic, she had been asleep for two months.

So much had happened in that time! For a while, the biggest and strongest were the ones admired. Eventually, the intelligent who managed not to be put to death by their governments achieved that admiration. The rich took over the spotlight for a week or so. Sports heroes, movie stars, and musicians also had their time.

Now all admiration fell upon those who were great to take walks with, to enjoy lion tamers with, and those who knew how to have fun with wax. Fred had become the ultimate human. He was fortunate enough to have all these traits and had the foresight to include them on his résumé to let the world know.

Henrietta tried to get through the crowd and say something to Fred, but he didn't recognize her with her shortened earlobes. Still, her smile once again attracted him and they were together that night. It was Henrietta who had ended their relationship years ago and she was happy that fate had given her another chance.

Three weeks later, all that was Fred was no longer in vogue. The current thing was being a trombone player with altered earlobes. Henrietta was the most popular person around while Fred faded into obscurity. Henrietta had the opportunity for a second chance to end her relationship with Fred and made use of it.

Fred never saw Henrietta again. He never called up the lion tamer and avoided walks in the park and anything to do with wax. He concentrated his efforts instead on imitating Eskimo morticians, wearing garlic suits, and defacing walls with Portuguese graffiti. This would, he believed, give him another chance at glory, although it made meeting women difficult.

Henrietta made the most of her fame, which was fortunate since it too was fleeting. She married the lion tamer and now lives happily in the suburbs. She no longer plays the trombone, since it is somewhere in her closet underneath many layers of wax.

No No No

The plane lost altitude quickly and Greta clutched her *Cosmo* pretending it was the Bible. She closed her eyes and thought about the green fields of Kansas where Aunt Mathilda and Uncle Umberto would be busy with their helpers, Stanley, Martin, and Cuddles, all working near a farmhouse in a beautiful bright orange against the open blue skies. And now this.

There were a few shrieks and some sobbing as Greta realized she would never go to Kansas and find out if there really were people there with the names she had just assigned. She whispered intensely, "No no no."

The plane lifted to where it had been, to where it was supposed to be. There were sighs all around the plane as all was back to a usual mundane okayness. Greta wondered how much she had influenced the forces that be to alter the plane's flight. Perhaps this entitled her to some money from each of the passengers who wanted to show their gratitude for their lives.

The cab home ran a red light and a large trash truck was headed for it at great speed. There seemed no way to avoid an accident as Greta closed her eyes again. She whispered, "No no no," and braced for the impact.

She heard some screeching and when she finally looked outside, the cab was about a half a block from the intersection. The driver turned to her to see if she was all right.

"Did you whisper, 'No no no'?" inquired the driver. "I think you saved my life."

The driver decided to show his gratitude by reducing the fare by a full thirty percent. She smiled and thought about how she would spend her $5.80 windfall.

She was alone at home later that night when she smelled smoke. She ran from room to room to search for the fire. There it was. There were flames in the kitchen from the floor to the ceiling. The fire was growing and heading for the can of gasoline she had left by the sink when she cleaned out her garage. Disaster seemed unavoidable. She closed her eyes and whispered, "No no no."

When she opened her eyes the fire was gone. Not only that but all traces of the fire were gone... except for the ashes from a fruitcake her boss had given her for Christmas a few years back. The fire had solved the problem of dealing with it.

Greta was lying on her bed and smiling with her eyes closed. It was a pretty special day. She had become a hero with wondrous powers. She planned to change her résumé in the morning to reflect those changes.

The doctor and nurse came in to Greta's room to check on her. The nurse couldn't understand the reason Greta was smiling as she slept. After all, Greta was in an airplane that hit a dump truck on the runway and as a result had some pretty bad burns. She asked the doctor how someone so unlucky could smile as she slept in her hospital bed.

"Some people save up all their luck for their dreams," replied the doctor.

Spiritual Virgin

She talked of walking through my hallways, late at night while my covers are clutched. She and I each in our beds so far apart and she wanders to me and into me. Still miles away, she talks in my ear and searches files and opens drawers. I don't understand how, but she was in me as I slept.

My doors are locked; she has a key. She scales walls and turns to watch them shrink to sizes she can step over when she tiptoes back to catch the sky. I didn't hear her last night but she knew the things I had hidden. I know she did. The locks are missing.

And deep in the darkened office of my mind is a filing cabinet so dark, dirty and musty that it kept out all intruders by its appearance. I awoke to find my folders sorted and the office clean enough for me to see what I had hidden. I need not hide from her. I have nothing left to hide.

Perhaps she can – perhaps she can't. I feel she did and that's what I know. I've never had one so deep within me. I lived as a spiritual virgin.

As the times toss me in directions uncharted, her voice gives focus. Her touch can pull me in. She leads, I follow. I always thought I charted courses, but I realize I've never seen the face of my pilot. Whoever steers me has given me all I need, at least since I've known her.

I wonder how many steps ahead she is. How many turns is she waiting for me to make to reach her? It doesn't matter. I follow with a new dedication.

Before the Grand Equator

Three more than planned, the musket stood before the Grand Equator who surveyed the pocket lilies of the northbound in the field. The circumference of the forest was the bolder of the sonnets and thus was given preference by the keeper of the wheel.

"Plow hearty, mean and nasty," said the now-revealed Equator who before the second chapter taught the priceless how to kneel. The Lady of the Trumpets pled her best to curse the misfits of the garden, with a plumber, sad and real.

She at once recalled the silence of a novice in a Plymouth who outdistanced snare and drummer to display the primal shield. All the time, the Grand Equator had emancipated wenches with a drop cloth and a satchel, and she had to change her stanza if but just to wax its seal.

The Zesty Saints

There were three of them. I counted them as I stared through the peephole of my front door, missing the culmination of the Dolphins' second half opening drive. The words I had initially planned to use to ward off this Sunday morning disturbance faded as I stared.

I opened the door and they stood and looked at me. The tall one wore a white suit with a pink shirt and a tie decorated with embroidered bananas. The short, round one had a hairstyle I vaguely remember seeing back in the '50s on the poster on the local barbershop wall. I'd never met anyone who actually chose that look before.

There was a third one. I know that there was. I just can't remember what he looked like. I think his name was Franko. He may have had glasses. The tall one was named Edgely and the short man with the memorable hair was Fabian.

Actually, that's not completely true. Each of them introduced themselves with the title of saint. "St. Edgely, that's my handle," said the tall one, which broke the awkward silence. St. Fabian told me his "moniker" and St. Franko (that sounds more correct each time I say it), St. Franko shared his, his whatever synonym he used.

"I'm taller than these other two saints," Edgely said. "Did you notice that right off? Most people do."

I nodded as Fabian added, "Some people wonder what it means to be in harmony with the city. Look, here is my bus schedule. It is still fairly accurate. Not many changes in two years."

There was a great deal of cheering coming from my television and I tried to remember whether the game was in Miami or New Orleans. Franko told me that the 2:30 bus was his and asked if he could sit quietly in my bathroom until then.

I decided to invite them in. I should have been in church anyway. After all, it was Sunday and there was a time when I would have been seated in the same pew on any Sunday. Perhaps these three were real saints as they claimed. More likely, they would serve as my penance for missing church services for years.

Edgely sat in my easy chair and started eating my toast. Fabian stood in the corner and raised his arms toward the heavens, or at least toward the cobweb above him. I could hear Franko chanting in the bathroom.

"Why are you visiting me on this beautiful Sunday morning?" I inquired.

"We are the Zesty Saints," Fabian replied. "It is our mission, our reason for being. What is your reason for being?"

"I work in a department store," I answered. "It's just temporary, until I can find something with a newspaper."

Neither Fabian nor I liked my answer. He shook his head and I was trying to figure out why my response seemed so flat. Edgely was staring at the television through the crust outline of the toast. Making the most of the acoustics of my shower, Franko was singing something that sounded like a fast food jingle.

"That is your reason for being?" inquired Fabian. There was a long silence, except for the Broadway show tunes that Franko had started rendering in the bathroom. "You could have said 'sunsets' or 'butterflies' or even 'blue Corvettes,' but you are like a worker bee or an ant stuck in a drab existence."

The Dolphins were ahead 17-0 by this point so I gave up on the game and offered my guests some cheese. I decided to unwrap the camembert that I was saving in the hope that Julie would see the error of her ways and come back and do my laundry. I reached for a bottle of merlot, paused, and put my hands behind my head. I really should ask first.

"Do you Zesty Saints drink wine!?" I shouted.

"We are modern people, so of course we do," shouted one of them impersonating another one of them, so I don't really know who responded. "The only thing we find morally reprehensible is camembert."

I was soon in my living room with four glasses of merlot and some Rolos. My television was now on the World War II Channel. Fabian and Edgely were standing on my coffee table, transfixed by the battle footage.

For some reason, seeing the two of them standing on my coffee table, staring at Rommel's troops in action made me feel a tad uneasy. Hearing Franko's loud attempts to hum the theme from *2001: A Space Odyssey* in my shower didn't make the situation any better. I decided some course of action was necessary.

I set the wine and Rolos down on top of the television and I turned the football game back on. I went into the kitchen and turned the hot water on full blast. I waited for the still showering Franko to notice how feeble my water heater was. I waited for five minutes before turning the water off and confronting the Zesty Saints.

I was very quiet as I approached the doorway to my living room. I could hear no sound beyond the last of the water droplets finding its way down the kitchen drain. The Zesty Saints were gone. I felt a great relief.

I took inventory. I had some wine left, as well as all of my camembert and even a few Rolos. Somehow New Orleans had made a comeback and the game on TV was tied and worth watching again. I decided that the next day, I would take my portfolio in to my cousin's ad agency.

All was suddenly right in my life. I felt blessed.

I Hate You for the Trees

And through the haze, I saw a village
I will settle here
This is where I was a child
This is where I was once happy
I will settle here

Alas, the village wouldn't have me
I was soon sent on my way
Another false promise
Another false hope
I was soon on my way again
Wiser and more confused
But more important, no longer alone
A maiden from the village now at my side

She held my hand and helped me leave
She held me tight and helped me stand
She gave me direction and made my lunch
And taught me how a bridge is built
She sheltered me and kept me warm

Twenty years later, the village dreams long gone
The maiden is still beside me
The years have not been easy
The years have not been kind
She should have left, I should have left
Our exits would have been quite just
But we are still as one, even closer
I know my reasons
I asked her for hers and she explained

"I love you for our hazy sky
I love you for each day's promise
And the carpet shared and bills we pay
And the nights we toast to better times
As we lock the door and stay inside

When we each could have run without blame

"I love the way you dream
And the way our souls link through our eyes
And that our words express the other's heart
I love you for the magic that lifts me
And the cleaning up you do after you cook

"I love you for all you are
We are one more than we are two
I love you for the roses your heart sends me
But I hate you for the trees"

The trees confused me
I again felt the haze of being alone
And heard the different tone in her voice

"You angered me and I threw seeds at you
You should have known that my heart hadn't changed
You should have felt my love through my walls
I should be able to change toward you without you reacting
In ways that make you change

"Instead you threw the seeds out the window
Where they landed in the rain-soaked soil
Where they grew into trees
I hate you for the trees
I love you with all the love I have
But I hate you for the trees"

And through the window, I saw our yard
The trees she spoke of had withered and died many years before
But they lived on in her mind
And that made them real and put them between us

I stared away and she brought me back
To the matters before us

"Don't drift away because you can't

Our souls can never separate
You are my one and all, my everything
You have my heart and my hands and my kitchen

"I love you for the life we share
The way you try to fight the haze
The way you hold and touch and give
I love you for all time

"I love you for the heart you share
I love the way we sleep
I love your eyes that bring me so close
But I hate you for the trees"

What Rebecca Knew

Rebecca knew that the man behind her couldn't really be a pirate. After all, she did live in Minnesota. She was an intelligent girl, not very easily fooled. But when she saw Queen Elizabeth I dub him a knight, poor Rebecca was greatly shaken.

Good Things Come in Sharp Packages

"Good things come in sharp packages," said the woman with the dated hairdo to the only one near the store display slow enough to listen. "This could be a nifty opportunity to buy something precise."

The slow one searched her mental files for a question to cast some light on those statements but came up lacking. She reached for her pocketbook and made the suggested investment.

"Now whatever you do with your acquisition, do it twice," said the woman in the dated hairdo. "If it was me, I'd have been you for those moments at least a couple of times before."

The slow one lit up for a moment, indicating that briefly she was on the logical track constructed by the other woman's statements. Regrettably, the brightness quickly flickered and burned out.

"Perhaps I could help you better understand my plan for creative living if I carried something of possible value into the midst of your most frequently forgotten concepts," continued the one with the dated hairdo. "In my last couch, I left a belt for an extinct toaster. Can we try something like that before the elves borrow your windows?"

The slow one smiled politely and followed the one with the dated hairdo out of the store and to the parking lot.

"There is a car in the lot that will take us to your possessions if we had the key," said the one with the dated hairdo. "Have you a key?"

The slow one looked in her purse and found a key. Through trial and error, a car matched the key and they were soon on the road. The scenery was wonderful as the weather highlighted all that nature and man had battled to create. Each woman was deep in her own thoughts, as well as they were capable of.

The car stopped in front of a large yellow house. The slow one produced a key that didn't match the lock in the front door, but again through trial and error, the women found a house it matched halfway down the block and the slow one was truly home.

"This is a nice place to live if you happen to have to live here," said the one in the dated hairdo. "For myself, I prefer to live somewhere where my own stuff is, although you have a nice recliner in your driveway. May I watch it through this window for a while?"

The slow one went to the room where the moving men had placed the electrical appliances years before and brewed some tea. The two women drank the tea and looked at the sharp package that had been placed on the floor in the middle of the room. They looked at each other and nodded and smiled.

"I do believe that the sharp package will prove to be amazingly enjoyable for you, unless you open it and are disappointed that there were no clues with it," said the woman in the dated hairdo.

The slow one decided that she wouldn't open the package right away so she could enjoy looking at its tight wrapping with the anticipation of what it was without risking emotional disappointment.

"You could be disappointed, what with all of the thoughts running through your uncluttered mind of what it could be and what fun it could be and the like," said the one with the dated hairdo. "Better keep it under wraps."

"But how will I ever get enjoyment out of my purchase?" asked the slower one.

"I can visit you every day and together we can look at the sharp package and speculate about what's in it," responded the one in the dated hairdo. "We can gossip about it – occasionally even cast some serious aspersions about what is in the sharp package. This will be better than opening the package because we can sit and watch it and talk about it forever, or at least as long as your refrigerator has food in it."

The woman with the dated hairdo came over every afternoon to watch the sharp package with her slow friend. They shared speculations and gossip about it. After about six months, the woman with the dated hairdo – actually, in six months, her hairdo became the rage again – moved in so they could spend more time talking about the package.

It was about fifteen years later when on a sunny May morning, the woman whose hairdo was once again outdated died. Over the next few weeks, temptation to finally open the package was too much for the slow one who was even slower with each passing year. She planned to rip the package open on a July afternoon but she didn't have the strength. She decided to take a nap but never woke up.

The sharp package was among the objects auctioned off by the city and it wound up in the hands of a shop owner who decided to offer it for sale without unwrapping it. Many customers have looked at it and wondered about it, but as of today, the sharp package is still tightly wrapped.

Glumness of the Alumni

The sniffling had been concluded. Fudgeworthy stood his ground. Clouds resembling Malaysian envelopes covered the sky around the blue building. Someone coughed.

The pirate mask had fallen from the eyebrows of the Norwegian beauty. She was tall. Really tall. Sheldon asked if there was an elevator to his favorite planet.

White shoulders rested on the back of the velvet drapery. Their owner was duly noted and transferred into a waiting bag. This was a night to be documented.

The next occurrence of any note was the buffalo stampede through the foyer. The glass was mercifully avoided and most of the china survived. Someone stirred his drink with a finger and wondered where he had wasted his previous twenty years. Debbie was drunk and surrounded by people named Oscar.

"Rosebud is the answer!" said someone paid to know better. Applause followed just the same. Nobody cared. Most just wandered. The magic had left them on a hot June night most of their lifetimes ago.

Ronald shuffled the cards and handed Ellie a number from one to ten. Weldon became a Buick that was quickly devalued. This was a night and not a smile in the bunch.

The years had come and gone. The milk had been spilled across the collective linoleum of life. Sighing abounded and somebody squeezed Flo's hand a tad too tightly. The punch soon gone inspired many to do the same. Their lives had peaked and only now was it all coming home.

Most would be back for their thirtieth...

The Amazing Salad of the Future

"Order the special," everybody told Loretta when she announced her plans to try out the new Space Palace. She was anxious to be there for the grand opening and was happy for the advice. It never occurred to her that since she was to be among the first to try the restaurant, her friends' advice had no credibility. She should be the one to give advice, and then only after testing the place herself.

Loretta ordered the special, which was called "The Amazing Salad of the Future." She finished about half of it, turned to me and said, "I'm afraid this is as far as I go in this story. Look over there at the next table, the couple with the toupee. Write about them instead."

I looked at Loretta and the keys of my typewriter kept clicking away.

"Hey!" she said, "I told you not to write about me anymore!"

My typewriter keys kept clicking.

"I'm leaving!" she announced. She left through the Jefferson Street exit and called a taxi. She climbed in. I was in the trunk, my typewriter still clicking. She seemed to notice because she got out quickly and hitchhiked. A large blue van with three tough-looking leather types picked her up. She was in no real danger since I was also in the van, still typing away.

"Damn! I thought I left you in the taxi trunk," she cried out. She was relieved when she found herself near home. The van pulled over and she ran up her front steps and locked her door.

"Would you like some of this pizza?" I asked her as she looked up to find me in her kitchen. She stared at me, still at my typewriter. She made a phone call and snuck out of her bedroom window. The taxi took her to the airport. She flew to Tonga in the first class section. The bus met her at the airport in Tonga and whisked her off to the Hilton Hotel.

She checked in and I tipped the bellman.

"Where did you come from?" she asked. "I thought I left you back in my apartment kitchen."

"Okay, I give up," she said. "If you want to write about me you can do it. What do you want from me?"

I looked up at her. She had proven to be worth following. "Actually nothing," I said. "This story is done."

Fluting Hippopotamus

There was music coming from the bushes behind the bench when our pal Edgar decided to go have a look-see. What he saw gave him a startle since he was not privy to the foreshadowing of this story's title.

Yes, it was a hippopotamus, and yes, the hippo was playing a flute. Edgar stared at the musical hippo and decided that he wanted to tell the world about what he had seen. No, better yet, he would take the hippo with him and make plans to travel the world and make a fortune with him.

Edgar escorted the hippo to his tiny apartment, which was on the third floor until the hippo entered it. He surveyed the damage, but hey, what's a few thousand dollars of damages when this hippo would be worth millions to him?

He drove the hippo to a talent agent and contracts were quickly signed. Edgar didn't need to read the contracts through. He saw a lot of zeros and that was good enough for him.

As it turned out, the hippo was worth a fortune because not only could he play the flute, he could talk. The hippo made millions in movies, television shows, and recordings. The money, however, all went to the hippo. Nothing went to Edgar.

Edgar looked back over the contract and indeed, the contract called for all of the money the hippo made to go to the hippo. Edgar decided to go and have a talk with him.

"I should get money because I discovered you," Edgar said to the hippo, who was seated behind a marble-topped desk in his penthouse apartment.

"Edgar baby, you have it all wrong," said the hippo as a bikini-clad bimbo lit his cigar. "I discovered you. You had no hopes, no dreams, and no ambitions until I came along. For a while, I made you feel happy and alive.

"I discovered the flute and I learned to play it, by myself, I may add," added the hippo. "I taught myself to read and to talk and to understand what to look for in a contract."

"Oooh, you're so smart," said the bimbo in the bikini.

"But look what you're doing with the money," Edgar continued his case. "You're wasting it. You have a penthouse, so I know you spent a bundle reinforcing the floors and building your own industrial elevator. You have a helicopter on the roof, twelve small sports cars, which I know you can't possibly fit into... and look at all of the junk you have in here. And look at these bimbos hanging around you. Do you really want to be with bimbos who would show affection to a hippo?"

"That's the best I can possibly get," the hippo responded logically. "Besides, what would you do with the money I made?"

"Probably the same thing you're doing," responded Edgar.

After a long pause, Edgar tried a different angle.

"Look at what you are becoming," said Edgar. "You are shallow, materialistic, and you have no personality anymore. You are now a pain to be with."

"Better me than you," responded the hippo.

Edgar thought for a while and walked out of the hippo's penthouse. He decided that maybe he was better off without all of the money. He wouldn't want to be as unlikable as the hippo had become. The simple pleasures in life were the best, he realized, because they didn't turn you into someone you wouldn't like.

Edgar wandered back to the park and sat on his favorite bench. He looked briefly into the bushes where he had first seen the hippo and heard his music. He turned back around and decided to concentrate on life's simple pleasures. He watched kids playing, birds flying, and lovers holding hands. He heard the noises of a baseball bat hitting a ball, children laughing, and harp music.

"Harp music?" wondered Edgar. He looked between the bushes and there where he discovered the hippo, was a rhinoceros playing a harp. Edgar thought for a moment.

"I'll bet you can talk, too," Edgar said.

"As a matter of fact, I can," replied the rhino. "How did you know? Most people wouldn't expect a rhino to talk."

Edgar and the rhino chatted for a while and they took a drive to the talent agent's office. After brief negotiations, Edgar looked over the contracts carefully before they were signed. Afterwards, Edgar and the rhino went to a local bar to celebrate with a drink.

"Edgar, the one thing I can't quite figure out is why you only asked for a small amount of the money I'll be making," said the rhino as he sipped his wallbanger.

"I have learned a great deal recently about the value of money and the value of the simple pleasures in life," Edgar responded. "I know what I need in life to make me truly happy. All I want for the time I spend working with you is enough to make me happy."

"Now I understand why you added the clause about you getting first pick of the bimbos," said the rhino.

They laughed, shared a few more drinks and looked forward to what life had in store for them.

Moral: The best things in life may be free but read carefully before you sign anything.

The Kamchatkan Tickling Episode

Unlike the moods that passed through Milwaukee Sam during the Eskimo shenanigans, the lack of lettuce in the Frigidaire was more ego-challenging. The sun was lower in the horizon then and those days had long since become blurred and blended with thoughts of the Himalayan trek. The lettuce, however, was a clear and present problem. Milwaukee Sam stood in the kitchen of the duplex with his unfinished sandwich open and ready.

Milwaukee Sam closed up the sandwich and wrapped it in a low-cost, imitation Baggie. He went to his desk and took out his folder of postcards received from people with last names from F to N. The sun was high in the sky and reflecting off the gloss of the postcards. It didn't matter. His eyes were closed.

Milwaukee Sam thought about his teenage days and the time that he took the flight into Pittsburgh on a dare. The Quaker incident had left a scar but he was happy that the years had eased his pain. He remembered Sally's face and the time they tried so hard to identify the animal that was eating their kite.

The cards from his friend in Poland made him wonder why someone had pulled out the camera in front of such buildings. The photographs she sent were much more interesting. They should have been the subjects of postcards. Unfortunately, his mind wandered to the days of the Lithuanian boot panic.

Milwaukee Sam's stomach growled and he considered the lettuce-less sandwich. He knew that within fifteen minutes he would give in. That's the way it always happened. Whether it was an incomplete sandwich or last summer's Indonesian courtyard challenge, it only took Milwaukee Sam a quarter of an hour to fold up and give in.

There was a book on the shelf that he didn't recognize and it distracted him. The sun was a little lower than before but not much. The book was on the Kamchatkan Tickling Episode and Milwaukee Sam decided to take the book to bed that night.

The sandwich was eaten, the postcards were put back into the folder and the folder was put away. The situation caused by the wrong water in Morocco would also be resolved before the sun set.

That night, Milwaukee Sam read the book about the infamous tickling and, until he realized the next morning that he was down to his third-favorite flavored coffee creamer, all the influences on Milwaukee Sam's peace of mind would be positive.

Pretzel Planning

Denton did the dishes while Miss Molly drew out her plans for the perfect pretzel. This was a Friday evening and all was right in their corner of the world.

Miss Molly called for Denton's assessment of her most current pretzel design and he dried his hands and went to where she was seated. He stared long and hard at her drawing and smiled politely. Her newest attempt simply wouldn't do and Denton struggled to become Miss Molly's source of truth.

"Sorry, my buttercup, this won't do," Denton said with all the love he could show in his eyes. "Somehow, you've left no room for the salt."

"These are supposed to be salt-free, you tweezerbrain!" replied an angry Miss Molly. "You just aren't interested in anything I do, are you?"

Somehow an argument was upon them, one that caught Denton off guard but one that was overdue for Miss Molly. He returned to finish the dishes before any words escaped him that would be difficult to clean up later. Miss Molly was angry that Denton had left yet another situation unresolved.

Denton had been honest with Miss Molly. He gave her his opinion when she asked for it. He even was nice and sweet and diplomatic. How was he supposed to know the pretzels were supposed to be salt-free? He would have jumped at the chance to apologize but simply could not find anything to apologize for.

Miss Molly stared at the stuffed alligator Denton had bought her the week before. It was cute but seemed to stare off in one direction only. It had a great deal in common with Denton, decided Miss Molly. It, like Denton, was unable to turn its attention to Miss Molly when she needed it. Her love for Denton had taken over her life and she was no longer close enough to anyone else who could give her the proper criticism of her pretzels.

Miss Molly had more to be angry about than Denton had to apologize for. Someone had to make a move and eventually would. After all, there was love there somewhere.

Queen Senator and the Pond

Queen Senator leaned over the railing of a balcony as I hovered high above her. There were flowers in the trenches and daisies in a bowl. I was looking for the pond and I needed to travel farther.

Sudden Mister flew off the handle as his Buick skidded. Sad tomatoes held their ground in a wooden box in the corner. I shouldn't look through windows. I know better. I have been there before. I should stay focused. I should be seeing water soon.

Toward the sandcastle was a waiter dressed in maroon shirt and black pants. Cleaning up for a party of twelve, he looked at the clock on the wall. I looked beyond and thought I saw water. I thought I heard splashing.

I went through one cloud and Queen Senator was well represented in the image of another. It could have been a dance, a bouquet, maybe even something from the bottom of the menu where the good stuff is mentioned. I hovered and traveled on. I saw a brook and decided to see where it emptied.

A line of imitation dancers filled a screen as cars passed by. A helicopter circled over them and I flew through the center of its noisy circle. The pond was ahead and I was at play. I sailed through the sky like I was on a rollercoaster. The moon soon caught my attention and I resumed my direction. I thought about the faces that had stolen my time. I thought about Queen Senator and felt myself losing altitude.

It didn't matter. There was a pond ahead. It would be beautiful. The moon was lighting it up. It would be a diamond to look down on. The dark that surrounded it would hide the bugs and icky things that keep many of us from automatically jumping into glittering water.

It was still ahead. It was in my flight plan. It was in my future. It was also in my past. My mind flickered back to Queen Senator and I thought about how cold the pond would be at night when I was about to approach. The brook became a path and I had been along this path before.

I thought about family and friends and debts and bad checks. I thought about books bought and unread. I looked back to where I had taken flight and couldn't tell where it was. There were buildings where there had been empty lots. There were children sleeping who weren't me. There was once a lake on a bed of concrete, but it was long gone.

Queen Senator was on a billboard – a billboard I almost hit. Or maybe that almost hit me. The brook was below it and I felt I could reach the pond without looking back again.

The waiter would be out of his carpeted prison by now. Whatever tomatoes were left in the box would have to be thrown out. Nothing worth a second flight. Nothing worth turning back for.

The brook became a stream and I could hear it from high above. The stream became a river. There was a Buick in the river and Sudden Mister stood on the shore and said things I couldn't hear. I felt good. I felt cocky. I swooped down to fly under a wooden bridge. I emerged and ascended and looked to find myself in a desert. Miles away, Queen Senator found the pond and it froze over. She dove in anyway and awoke in a hospital bed.

I wanted to go home. The best I could do, however, was find a place and make it home. I knelt in a doorway. The door opened and I slept on the floor. When I awoke, I heard a splash.

There was a pond in the living room of a home I once slept through. There were tomatoes in the freezer and reservations on a note on the coffee table. There was an old queen with a new smile, and she welcomed me back with open arms and angry eyes.

I don't know where Queen Senator is living. And I don't care how or even why. The joke is on the others. My wings aren't strong enough to carry me away again.

Garbage Defeats Love

A mug of frosted ale in the hands of someone large and obnoxious was the first thing Dee noticed when she walked into the Girth and Brew. She was there to meet someone who looked good in a three-piece suit. Fredo was not the kind of person one would look at twice during the ordinary run of things. He was short and thin and was missing a strategic tooth. But in a three-piece suit, he was able to alter Dee's opinion of him enough to get a yes from her when neither one of them really expected it.

Fredo was nowhere to be seen so Dee looked at her watch. She was four minutes early and decided to sit at a table. A tall weatherworn waitress walked over to her.

"What will you be having?" she asked Dee.

"I'll have what that man over there is having," Dee said, pointing to the man with the mug of frosted ale.

"I wish you hadn't said that," said the waitress as she snapped her fingers and pointed at Dee. The bartender walked over to throw her out the side door.

"That man over there is going to be thrown out of here as soon as we get another person to help us," he told her. Dee unfortunately didn't hear him, choosing instead to focus on the trashcans she was rapidly approaching.

She stood up a moment or two after the landing to take inventory of the damages. Fredo was standing beside a nearby fence, doing the same thing as he surveyed the damage to his three-piece suit.

"I guess you ordered what I ordered," Fredo said, smiling. "Come on, I know a better place."

"Fredo, look at your three-piece suit," said Dee. "It's ruined."

"I guess I'll have to stop by my place and change," he said.

"No, that won't do. I'm very sorry, Fredo, but without that suit I have no interest in being with you."

"But Dee, I have been dreaming of being with you for a long time."

"I'm sorry, Fredo."

"Dee?"

"What is it, Fredo?"

"Why is there tissue coming out of your blouse?"

Dee looked down to find that the tissue she had so carefully stuffed her bra with had come loose. She was embarrassed.

"Dee, I'm afraid that I agree with you on calling our date off. If the reasons I had for being with you are actually only tissue, I have no interest in being with you."

As it happened, Dee and Fredo were parked next to each other in the lot of the Girth and Brew. They didn't look at each other as they got into their respective cars and drove in their separate directions. They would never attempt another date with each other.

Quite a shame since they had so much in common.

Buchanan Returns for His Change

It was thirty minutes past the hour when the sedan pulled to a stop by the five and dime. A man in a suede suit strolled into the phone booth. He looked into the coin return tray. There it was. His twenty cents had been returned.

When he had left the booth an hour before, he was too concerned that his call was unanswered to remember that his two dimes would fall into the tray. He was a worrier and lately seemed paranoid.

He found a quarter underneath his dimes. He wondered who else had used the phone booth. Was it someone else who had tried to call her also? He became a victim of his paranoia.

He got back into his sedan and drove to the theater. He saw a movie or two and felt all better. At least for the time being.

Yak #347

Yak #346 was on his deathground. Summoning up his remaining strength, he looked at the young yakface that stood over him.

"My son, it's all over for me," said the dying yak between dramatic coughs. "The time has now come for you to carry on the yak tradition in this valley. Yak forth throughout the valley and into the forests and through the marshes. You are Yak #347 and our legacy is in your hands... or hooves... you know what I mean."

With that, Yak #346 became history. Yak #347 walked away and started living a life that would have made his father proud. He did his yak thing all around the valley. All other creatures big and small looked at him and knew that this was indeed a yak. There was no mistaking him for a sparrow or a cat or a beautician.

One day, however, the mailman brought Yak #347 a long-awaited letter. Southern State offered him the football scholarship he had hoped for. The school offered courses in everything that Yak #347 needed to grow as a yak.

There was a problem, however. The school team name was the "Non-Yaks." This posed a dilemma for Yak #347. By pursuing his dreams, he would be forced to deny his own yakhood. He thought long and hard for the next several minutes before deciding to take the scholarship.

He played as a member of the starting defense for three years at Southern State while he studied and learned and became the best-educated yak on record. He looked forward to his senior year when he would have the chance to be at his best for his team.

And then it happened.

One of the players who had graduated that summer wrote a book. Amid the accusations of drugs, steroids, gambling and promiscuity of the other players were two sentences, in black and white, for all the world to see:

"Yak #347 is really a yak. I know because I had the locker next to his."

Calls and letters from angry alumni flooded the coach's office. Essentially their complaint was the same. "A yak simply cannot be a Non-Yak."

Yak #347 was thrown off the team and sent home. He was grateful, nonetheless, that he had a chance to learn in the three years he was there. He knew what yaks needed to lead more fulfilling lives. Alas, this created more problems for Yak #347.

When he returned to the valley, he knew that the vegetation was not as good for yaks as it was about thirty miles to the north. He tried to be happy with what the valley offered him, but he knew too much. He grumbled and complained and found fault with everything around him. He finally decided to travel the thirty miles to a better life.

It was on the bus ride to his new home that the words of his father played over and over in his head. "You are Yak #347 and our legacy is in your hands... or hooves... you know what I mean."

When the bus stopped, Yak #347 picked up his suitcase and walked out to the nearby hills. There he saw yaks of all descriptions. They were happy, they were healthy, they were enjoying the fullness of yakhood. There he met Yak #428.

She was beautiful. Their eyes met and it was love at first sight. Together they strolled through the hills, into the valley, through the marshes, and around the mall. Yak #347 knew that she was the yak for him. They soon married and had a little yak that they thought about naming Yak #347, Jr., but they decided on following family tradition and instead named him Yak #348.

Yak #347 should have been happy with his life. He had a beautiful wife and a son and he lived on what he found out was a refuge for yaks, which meant that the government paid for everything. Unfortunately, the words of his father played in his head and he felt that he had not followed his true purpose in life.

One night when there was no moon and the sky was very dark, Yak #347 started his journey back to the valley where he had grown up. He left a note for his family to read when they awoke.

Somewhere in the hills along the way there was a bridge that snapped when Yak #347 walked on it and he fell a great distance. Somehow after being unconscious for a long while, he was able to get up and continue his travel. He knew, however, that he was badly injured and continuing would probably cost him his life.

Still, he was determined to reach the valley he knew so well. If he could get there before he died, he believed that he would have somehow fulfilled the promise that he made years before to his dying father. It was a long and tough journey, but Yak #347 made it back just before he collapsed.

He lay on what he knew would be his deathground as his mind flickered between haze and reality. He opened his eyes and saw standing over him his wife and son.

"Why did you leave us?" asked his wife, the beautiful Yak #428.

"This is where I belong," responded Yak #347. "My father wanted me to be here and make sure that yaks were represented in this valley. I am so ashamed. When I was gone, first to school and then to your hills, this valley was yakless. Completely yakless! My father spent his entire life here keeping our traditions alive and I should have done the same."

"My dear husband," responded Yak #428, attempting to sugarcoat the obvious. "If he spent all his life here as the token yak, you would never have been born. My parents remember seeing him quite often in the hills that you just left. He even asked my mother out a few times, but she was dating my father at the time. Did you know that your father also had a football scholarship and that he went to a school that had the team name of 'Yak-Haters'?"

"Are you saying that I passed up a happy life in the hills to die here in this yakless valley?" asked Yak #347. "Am I dying in vain?"

Yak #428 said nothing but quietly bandaged her husband's legs and fixed him some Bosco. All the while, she was thinking of a response that her husband could handle. He looked at his young son's yakface and selected his words carefully.

"It seems that the traditions that have been passed down through the generations may sound great, but like every political and social system known to yaks, they have all been screwed up by yak weaknesses and frailties. You are Yak #348 and your legacy is to be Yak #348. Define it as you see fit."

Proud of his words and feeling somewhat better, Yak #347 managed to live for several more months. Although he stayed in the same place during that time, he was happy. A television was brought there for him to watch and he read several books on the meaning of life.

One book was based on the theory that yaks are sent to Earth to learn their lessons. Each yak has a particular problem to try to understand and solve. Those who have worked out the problem in their life have accomplished their goal. Although the solution may require a great deal of pain, there is always peace in understanding how everything fits together and, in the final level of understanding, you realize how everything is one big yak.

Episode Eight in Futility

Clark, at our last writing, was standing in the field behind a cow named Bruno, afraid to go into the house where Sara stood reading his note. The day was coming to a close. Milton was at his home, resting comfortably, unconcerned about being left out of this story.

A large ox was chewing hay nearby. Clark had been there for some time. Sara assumed he would come into the house sooner or later. Night fell.

The next morning found Clark still standing behind the cow. He was contemplating his options. The cow had no options. The sun was high in the sky.

The house needed painting badly, which qualified Sara's uncle for the job. After four days, the job was complete. Clark thought again about entering the house. His legs were tired and the house had a new inviting color. He also began to miss Sara. Night fell.

Sara went away to college where she lived for four years. She returned home and waved to both the cow and Clark. "Perhaps," thought Clark, "this would be a good time to make my move."

The ox had died. The cow was still strong, however, as were Clark's legs. He thought about leaving his spot in the field and entering the house. The years had taken their toll.

The next summer brought both heat and sunshine. Clark removed his coat.

Sara's wedding the following spring brought the entire town to her house. Her divorce six years later was more private. Clark stood watching through the changes. He thought again about entering the house. Night fell.

One winter day, the cow died. Clark went home.

A World without Pleats

Velvet watched some television but kept looking at the man she had committed herself to. Morris stared out the window to where the stars were. The city lights kept him from seeing anything but the moon and an occasional airplane, but he seemed to be concentrating more internally than externally.

She flipped the station to a music channel in the hope that the tune would bring Morris into the realities of the apartment. She pulled the hem of her blue robe to the borderline of the good stuff. He went to the computer and intensely typed something.

He got up after about five minutes and approached the curtains. He reached out his right hand and felt the pleats. He shook his head and once again he returned to his typing.

Velvet lowered her hemline and flipped to the news. There was more than the usual amount of blood pictured and she held a magazine in front of her face to keep the images away. When a commercial was on, she lowered the magazine to find that Morris was no longer in the room.

Before she made a decision about whether or not to find him, he returned. He was carrying a few hangers' worth of clothing. Some were his, some were hers, but all had one thing in common. All of them had pleats.

He set them down on the dining room table near the desk with the computer and studied each one in turn, walking back and forth to the computer to type out his observations. Velvet stared at Morris and found his efforts to be more entertaining than the sports segment. Besides, there was more than the usual amount of blood pictured in the sports segment.

"Imagine a world without pleats," Morris said to her and she gave his comment a moment's pondering, if only to compensate for his moment's attention.

"A world without pleats?" inquired Velvet.

"Yes, I'm afraid so," Morris said dejectedly. "All of the good ideas have been taken by the billions of people who proceeded me to the pens, typewriters, and computers on this planet. This 'world without pleats' concept may be silly and strange but it's all mine."

Velvet got up from the couch and turned off the television. She walked over to the dining room table where Morris stood surveying the garments. She stood behind him and put her arms around him.

She loved him and understood completely the meaning of his theory. He might be silly and strange but he was all hers. She would wait up for him in bed, even if his ponderings took hours.

Well, Be at Noon by Threeish

Lady Floogleman stood by her staircase and waited for someone she had recently hired to pass by her. That person eventually did, and she spoke in the direction she had been facing while waiting.

"Be a dear and walk to the stones and glory be to all for this wondrous day we had lunch in," she said regally. The recipient of the message responded with an "As you wish" and retreated to the book of Lady Floogleman translations. He returned ten minutes later with an alabaster and cheese on rye, and Lady Floogleman smiled and threw a tangerine at the painting of an ox with feathers.

The newly hired person was soon back at the book of translations. Flipping to the glossary of Lady Floogleman actions, he smiled. "A compliment, a mighty fine compliment indeed," he said to himself.

Not much time was allowed for him to bask in the glory of his accomplishment for he heard a Barry Manilow favorite being played at full volume at 78 rpm. Other than the aesthetic improvement, he wondered what significance could be gleaned from this act.

Page 349 had the answer and he quickly donned the lion outfit and went to greet Lady Floogleman. "Growl!" he attempted. "Grrr, grr, growl again!" he added.

Lady Floogleman was wearing a different color shoe on each foot. The boot was blue and the tennis shoe a nice shade of apricot. With one shoe she stood on her hired help's tail. But which shoe? That was the key.

He didn't turn around in time to see which shoe had stepped on the tail of his outfit. He thought for a moment but however he reacted, he had a fifty-fifty chance of responding correctly.

"My day was catered by an envelope of great cheers and soap suds, Lady Floogleman," he said and added, "Growl, yet again!"

Lady Floogleman sat on the steps and cried. His response was apparently wrong. It must have been the tennis shoe in the rather nice shade of apricot that stepped on his lion's tail. A turn of his head and the glimpse of the treadmarks on the tail confirmed his fears. He improvised a course of action.

"My dear Lady Floogleman, the mad beavers of Astoria stood on my ground as the first dimes of daylight flickered to the happy," he said somberly, trying to make his bottom lip quiver as if it were holding back his sobs. "Another hope of Thursdays unseen is my quest."

Lady Floogleman looked puzzled. She stood up and walked to the book of Lady Floogleman translations. This was one she hadn't used for a while. She returned and said, "Well, be at noon by threeish."

The hired person in the lion suit excused himself and consulted the Lady Floogleman book. Her response had been, "Yes, yes, a thousand times yes!"

He was tempted to find out what he had said to her. What could he have said which would get such a response? He thought again about the matter and decided that it might be more fun not to find out. He would return to where Lady Floogleman stood drawing targets on her elbows with her purple eyeliner.

She grabbed him by his lion ears and led him in a conga step through her house to the Eskimo Amusement Room between the pantry and the trolley depot. They lived happily ever after, except on alternate Wednesdays when the camels had the run of the hologram projection booth.

Walrusman Stands Tan for Number One

Superheroes need a break between the prison escapes of archrivals so Walrusman was enjoying the sun and sand of Kansas when his two big front teeth started vibrating. Someone was calling for his services.

"Stand tan for number one," he thought to himself. "Even you deserve a rest."

A few babes walked by and Walrusman's decision became clear. He would enjoy the sun, the sand, and the babes. He stayed a full week before returning to the big city.

After that, his teeth didn't vibrate for weeks. His telephone didn't ring. The police didn't seem to need his help anymore.

He went down to police headquarters as his alter ego, millionaire locksmith Wally Russman, to find out how things were going crimewise.

"Wally Russman, it's so good to see you again," said the police commissioner. "I wish I had time to talk to you but Devious Dave is on the loose. I need to place a call to the defender of our city, Broccoliman."

"Broccoliman?" inquired Wally.

"Yes, he's a good friend of wealthy sanitation engineer Brock Leeman," answered the commissioner. "Strange how they never seem to be in the same place at the same time."

"I'm gone for one week and some guy in a vegetable suit has taken my place," thought Wally. "No more dressing up as an awkward animal and risking life and limb for absolutely no pay."

Wally quickly realized that there were advantages to being free from his former civic duties. He was angry at having Broccoliman take his place, however.

Wally went home and left again as Walrusman. While Broccoliman fought the clever plans of Devious Dave, Walrusman put up some wire fences around the state prison, and installed locks on the cell doors. The warden was in awe of his cleverness. When Devious Dave was captured, nobody else would be able to escape from state prison.

It was about a month later when Walrusman was back on the sands of Kansas surveying the babes. He turned to his right and looked at Broccoliman.

"Stand tan for number one," Walrusman advised his new friend.

Broccoliman, however, was too distracted by the babes. He decided to make himself more attractive to them by putting on some butter.

The Silliest Rainbow

June 14: Was approached by Mssrs. Goldborough and Snuff regarding my knowledge of multicolored oddities. They attempted to set up an appointment that evening but it was my bowling night.

June 15: Was met early in the a.m. by the same two gentlemen who contacted me yesterday. They complimented my tie and threw three dead pigeons on my desk. Said they were found in the Northern Fields under a rainbow. The silliest rainbow they had ever seen. Or so they said.

June 16: Set out for the Northern Fields to find out the cause of the pigeons' demise. They had all apparently bumped something. Their bruises were each a different color. Had lunch.

June 17: Reached the Northern Fields. Found more pigeons with more different color bruises. Looked up.

June 18: Saw the silliest rainbow that I'd ever seen in my life. Actually, I saw it yesterday but I only now stopped laughing.

June 19: Was hit by a falling pigeon.

June 20: Had breakfast at a fast food outlet.

June 21: Went bowling.

June 22: Contacted a reporter from the local newspaper and told him about the silliest rainbow. He hung up on me.

June 23: Headed off to the newspaper office.

June 24: Reached the newspaper office and met with the reporter who had hung up on me. I threw a pigeon on his desk. Real drama building here.

June 25: He expressed an interest in accompanying me to the Northern Fields to see the silliest rainbow. He also expressed an interest in bowling.

June 26: Reached the Northern Fields, which had just become a tourist attraction. Dodged a falling pigeon.

June 27: Had lunch.

June 28: Bowling night. The reporter was also there.

June 29: Lectured at the local university about the rainbow. Threw five pigeons into the audience. They thought it was a great thing to do, just like a rock concert.

June 30: Approached Mssrs. Goldborough and Snuff to inquire whether or not I was to be paid for verifying the rainbow. They said no.

July 1: Admitted that the rainbow was a hoax, and that Goldborough and Snuff were very silly people.

July 2: Had dinner. Wrote my memoirs.

Jamaal, Alphonse, Edgar and An Unnamed Desk

Jamaal bought a large green filing cabinet, which he named Edgar. He wanted to have the cabinet at his left side during his working hours.

He bought a blue steel bookshelf, which he named Alphonse. This bookshelf, thought Jamaal, would be good to have with him at his right side at work.

He then purchased a desk, which remained unnamed because he ran out of favorite names. The desk would be in front of him at all times during work.

Unfortunately, Jamaal's work was being a trapeze artist. The details of the tragedy will not be discussed here.

Conquering the Curb

I painted my name next to your street number and although it's blurred, it's proof I've conquered the curb.

The Spaniard Stood in the Sandwiches

Helen and Bob Jordan were so pleased that all of the town's non-riffraff had responded in a positive manner to their invitations. All the who's who of a town that nobody outside of their state had heard of were there, sporting their finest spring fashions and enjoying the food at their afternoon party.

Spooning out the colorful coleslaw were the Blakes, Selma and Thaddeus, who were so well-to-do that they actually knew someone who shook hands with someone who attended the inauguration ceremonies for the first President Bush. Near them was Quincy McDonald, the self-made retiree, helping himself to something that resembled lasagna. The Charles sisters were loading up on those yellow things that look like corn embryos but taste like pickles.

And at the far end of the food was a strong and sturdy Spaniard standing in the quarter-cut sandwiches. With his armored breastplate and colorfully plumed helmet that would have made Cortés or Pizarro jealous, he lifted the Spanish flag he held and shouted, "I claim these sandwiches for His Majesty King Philip II of Spain! The Swedish meatballs look good too."

The Spaniard snapped his fingers and five other soldiers who, with their armor and plumed helmets, appeared to be his associates, emerged from the bushes. As they approached the Jordans' inspired food offerings, they pulled out their swords to keep the invited crowd at a distance.

The Spaniard who stood in the sandwiches stepped back into some squishy slices of something purple to the dismay of no one who tried the stuff. One of the soldiers grabbed the sandwich tray. A second poured the Swedish meatballs into his helmet. Another took the tuna casserole. Others took what remained of the more popular entrées and offerings – including a very elaborate punchbowl.

The Spanish forces ran off toward the Jordans' garage where they had hidden some horses. They rode off to a Seven-11 for drinks and then off toward the galleon that waited for them at the shore. The partygoers applauded politely, just in case this was an attempt by the Jordans to provide entertainment. It certainly was better than the accordion player at the Griffiths' recent pool party.

Somewhere in the middle of the Atlantic, a proud Spanish captain surveys the spoils of his victory against the Jordans – of which the tuna casserole was perhaps the most spoiled. The sandwiches, however, still looked good and the captain wondered if King Philip would knight him for his bounty. Perhaps his chances would be better if his footprints were not as recognizable. Ah, but the very elaborate punchbowl should impress his majesty.

But what's this? Another vessel approaches the Spanish ship just as it nears the Azores. The ship looked friendly enough, at least a little while ago. Gone now, however, is the flag that read "The Worst Day of Sailing is Better than the Best Day of Work." In its place is the Jolly Roger flag – the infamous skull and crossbones!

But these aren't your usual pirates. These aren't Blackbeards or Bluebeards or Redbeards who are attempting to board the Spanish galleon. No, look! It's the Jordans, Helen and Bob. Right behind them are their kids, Gail, Derek, and Wally.

Gail applauds as her mother runs somebody through with her sword. Bob, the leader of the Jordan clan, is making several of Madrid's finest walk the plank. The action is fast and furious. "This is even more exciting than Tuesday night television," thinks Gail. Wally is happy to do anything other than homework on a school night.

After the captain and crew had either been killed by the Jordans' swords or eaten by sharks, Helen looked over the things that had been taken from their party. She turned to her husband and said, "It's here! My very elaborate punchbowl is here. We haven't done all of this in vain."

Her spirits were saddened however when she noticed the chip at the top, but her husband reminded her that she had kept the receipt. "Yes! I can exchange it," said a once again gleeful Helen.

The Jordans decided to pass on the tuna casserole, instead taking all the gold and jewelry from the chest in the captain's quarters. They set fire to the ship before they left.

Helen Jordan was counting gold coins as their ship returned to Charleston Harbor. She smiled and thought about how nobody would give them problems at any of their afternoon parties ever again.

In fact, the group of Vikings who arrived in the Jordans' home state three months later picked on a barbecue thirty miles away instead.

Convincing Renee

Renee spent a good deal of her life trying to convince people that she was a tree. One day, her friends decided that maybe they should explain to Renee that she wasn't a tree.

After about a day and a half, her friends, using such visual aids as a match and a mirror, finally convinced her that she wasn't really a tree but rather a beautiful set of porcelain dishware.

Running Patterns of Squirrels

Wilhelm truly understood the deeper meanings behind the running patterns of squirrels. He could tell with a quick glance which were troubled and which were truly content. He had spent time, more time than one could comfortably imagine, developing his talent and he was unquestionably the best at what he did.

As things happened, however, there was little demand in his small town for his talent. Wilhelm decided to move to a midsize town to try his luck. Armed with a briefcase full of résumés, each heralding his squirrel running analytical abilities, he knocked on every door that could possibly have someone interested in his expertise behind it. When he ran out of doors, Wilhelm moved on to the big city.

As the DC-10 touched down in the metropolis, Wilhelm planned his attack. He would go to a copy center and replenish his résumé supply. He would find a hotel room with a yellow pages directory and make a list of every business that could possibly use him.

Alas, there was less interest in squirrel analysis in the metropolis than in his small town or in the midsize town. With all the building and expanding and traffic and noise of the big city, there were no squirrels left anymore. It took about a week for Wilhelm to realize this, although the day after he arrived, deep down inside he knew that his efforts would be in vain. Not only weren't the people in the metropolis interested in hiring him, they weren't even interested in hearing him. The hectic life of the big city kept those empowered to hire and fire folks from having enough time to hear what Wilhelm had to say. At least the people in the small town and the midsize town took time for the potential amusement involved in listening to him. Not those in the metropolis, however.

The end of the week found Wilhelm standing on a high ledge of a tall building looking at the busy street for a good place to land. He opened his briefcase and threw his stack of résumés into the air. As they fell, people looked up and saw Wilhelm on the ledge. It wasn't long before a crowd gathered and policemen had arrived; some on the sidewalk with mops and some leaning out of the windows nearest to Wilhelm, trying to lure him in to safety with cheese and chocolate cake.

A young police sergeant was soon sitting next to Wilhelm on the ledge of the tall building. The two talked calmly while they enjoyed some camembert.

"Your problems can't be all that bad," said the sergeant, "not bad enough to splatter yourself on the sidewalk."

"I have no purpose anymore," said Wilhelm calmly enough to give the sergeant confidence in his eventual success. "All I can do is analyze the running patterns of squirrels. I'm the best in the world at that, but it doesn't matter."

"Have you tried applying for a government grant?" inquired the sergeant.

"I'm not comfortable doing that," responded Wilhelm. "I was cursed with a conscience."

"Boy, look at that crowd," said the sergeant. "They look so small from up here. Look at them scurrying back and forth and look at how that crowd below us is growing."

"Oh, no!" shouted Wilhelm, which scared the sergeant. "Look over there, the three people with the moustache. They're about to rob the pawnshop across the street."

The police sergeant quietly watched the three people Wilhelm had pointed out. Within a minute, they were running out of the pawnshop, carrying sacks of money and some tacky clocks. The police sergeant looked at Wilhelm in awe.

"How did you know that?" he asked.

"I don't know," Wilhelm said. "I just knew. See that guy wearing the Mr. Bill T-shirt? He's about to hop over the mailbox, take two steps, turn, and push the man with the white shoes through the plate-glass window of the Finnish restaurant."

The police sergeant said something into his portable phone as he stared at the man in the Mr. Bill T-shirt. Everything happened just the way Wilhelm predicted and there were two police officers waiting to apprehend the man who had committed the crime Wilhelm had predicted.

The sergeant stared at Wilhelm for his next statement. There were a few minutes of silence, which made the sergeant uncomfortable. "How about those two guys in front of the otter shop?" he asked Wilhelm.

"They're Republicans," Wilhelm replied. "They won't do anything that your officers would need to be ready for. That would force them to interact with strangers.

"But look over there," he continued. "There is a pickpocket approaching the crowd below us."

Again, Wilhelm was right and there was another arrest. After a couple hours, the crowd below the ledge was gone. Many had given up hope in Wilhelm's demise. Many others were in police custody for crimes predicted by Wilhelm.

There were some rewards that went Wilhelm's way, but the main result of the day's events was that Wilhelm was hired by the metropolitan police department and given a penthouse office high in the building he almost jumped from. He was glad he hadn't jumped. He was happy that he didn't choose a permanent solution to his temporary problem.

He really should have known all along that things would somehow work out. People with special talents are eventually given a forum for those talents.

Yeah, right.

Cheerful Wet Bags of Clay

Cheerful wet bags of clay landed on my plateau on June's finest day as I was planting my silverware before the thaw. Couldn't have been more than an hour before some furry company was set to arrive that the thuds were heard. I simply couldn't relate to the clay.

Sedgewick stood in the doorway of the helicopter as I looked up, puzzled. He seemed to be offering a look of sympathy, remembering when he was almost a victim of the cheerful wet bags of clay. Now, however, it was my turn to cope. I read a book for inspiration.

I sent away for a shovel and put up signs to keep pickpockets at a distance. Honestly, it seems that vultures are always ready to strike when your airspace has proven vulnerable. I checked my calendar: the thaw was fast approaching and the spoons were still above ground. I called my company for the evening and they decided to stay home and shave.

The wet bags of clay were still cheerful despite my anger. Some Indians came by and wished me well. A bird landed on my patio armchair. The sun was approaching the horizon. Some nation invaded another. The Cubs lost a double-header. Life continued and the bags were still too gleeful for me to handle.

I took the wheelbarrow from the tool shed and bought a sledgehammer from my grandmother. Within an hour, my job was complete. I had enclosed the wet bags of clay behind a fence. They weren't cheerful now. Nope, not anymore.

I finished planting the spoons and had time to fix some popcorn before the thaw arrived. The cheerful wet bags of clay proved to be no match for me. No sir.

Keeping an Eye on Waldo the Great

Tripping happily along the hot sidewalk was Mr. Bannister, the last in a long line of happy-go-lucky sidewalk trippers dating back to the first sidewalks in Duluth. The current Mr. Bannister carried all of the Bannister traits. He was tall, blond, and used a very silly expression to convey his nonchalance.

Waldo the Great owned a small fix-it shop on the boulevard where Mr. Bannister was continuing family tradition. While Waldo the Great tended to enjoy the sounds of people walking back and forth along the pavement, there was something in the quirky rhythm of Mr. Bannister's footsteps that caused him to walk out of his shop and offer a few loud words.

"Where did you learn to walk?" was the first group of Waldo the Great's loud words.

"I didn't have to learn to walk," Mr. Bannister calmly responded. "Walking is in my genes."

"But you're wearing cords," said Waldo the Great.

"Not my pants type of genes, my heredity type of genes," clarified Mr. Bannister. "Through family traits that have been passed down from generation to generation, I walk the way I walk."

Waldo the Great went back into his shop to find a small appliance to hurl in the general direction of Mr. Bannister. Upon locating a thirty-year-old toaster, he grabbed it only to find that Mr. Bannister was now inside his shop standing very close to the large front window.

"Would you mind moving out to the sidewalk?" asked Waldo the Great politely. "I would like to hurl this toaster at you and I would hate to break my front window."

Responding to the politeness of the request, Mr. Bannister walked out to the sidewalk to have the toaster thrown at him. Not being a fool, Mr. Bannister walked backwards out of the shop to keep an eye on Waldo the Great.

Waldo the Great put the toaster down on a blue wooden rocking chair and shook his head. "That was beautiful," he thought and he asked Mr. Bannister to come back into the shop.

Mr. Bannister walked back into the shop, confused about why the toaster was now on a chair. Waldo the Great screamed and pounded his fist on the counter.

"No, you idiot, not like that!" shouted Waldo the Great. "Walk backwards again."

Mr. Bannister offered no complaints about the request. He was more than willing to walk backwards to once again keep an eye on the cranky repairman.

"That's it!" shouted Waldo the Great. "That's beautiful. Your steps are so melodic when you walk backwards. It's as if all the melody inside you paces your steps when you go backwards. Please do it again."

Mr. Bannister turned to face the door of the shop and walked backwards toward the counter. Upon hearing applause from Waldo the Great, he turned and walked backwards to the door. He repeated the process again and again.

After about half an hour of this, as Mr. Bannister walked backwards to the counter again, Waldo the Great hit him over the head with the toaster, killing him. After dragging his body behind the counter, Waldo the Great found Mr. Bannister's wallet and helped himself to a healthy amount of cash.

Waldo the Great dragged Mr. Bannister's body to a back room where it was placed on top of other bodies. Waldo the Great then walked to his front window to find his next customer.

Frozen Spider Evening

Helga walked into the Frozen Spider Restaurant and saw the current target of her heart. He was seated with another woman and Helga stood in shock for a moment before walking back outside.

"Jonathan, would you like to meet me for dinner at the Frozen Spider?" she said into a nearby pay phone to someone she knew would never decline a female invitation. "I'm here now."

With that done, Helga walked back into the restaurant and was seated at a table where she could keep an eye on Edwin, the current commodore of her caring, as he sat with another woman. She sat and stared and soon had an effect on the prime minister of her palpitations. Edwin was obviously distracted by her.

Edwin looked at Helga as she stared at him. He was confused for a moment. Helga was indeed the duchess of his deep desires, but Lynn, who was seated with him, was presently the naughty nanny of his nasty needs. It was then that he was shaken from his thoughts by Edna the waitress, the big bad bringer of his burned bacon lettuce and tomato.

Lynn took the opportunity of Edna's arrival to look around behind her and she recognized Helga. A photograph that Edwin had forgotten to put away led to Lynn's recent questioning about who she was and why she had signed the photo as "Your Fantastic Flower of Forbidden Fantasy." Lynn took a sip of wine and started her response to the situation.

"Dearest Edwin," she said, putting her wineglass on the table, "I chanced to look behind me at the woman at the far table and, lo and behold, I fear that it is none other than your barbaric buttercup of bitchiness."

"Well my darling dictator of daring desire, you are right," said Edwin. "I hadn't noticed her sitting there."

Edwin looked deep into Lynn's eyes to see if she bought that one. He decided to glance back and compare his former fountain of fantastic fun with his current catalogue of cuteness. It was then that Jonathan arrived.

"Egad," thought Edwin, "it's Jonathan, that obnoxious oval orangutan. What is he doing here with Helga?"

Lynn noticed Edwin's concern and turned around to take another look at Helga.

"Jealous, are we, my sneaky snake of slime?" inquired Lynn. "You made yourself my white knight of delight and now you look back at your past president of pukiness as if you have doubts. You are a... Hey, wait a minute! That's my Jonathan."

"Your Jonathan, my jaded jewel of jealousy?" asked Edwin. "And here I thought you were my tempting teapot of truthfulness."

"Just let me get my hands around the neck of that scrawny scoundrel of scum!" shouted Lynn as she stood up and walked over to Jonathan and Helga. Although she wasn't sure enough about her feelings toward Jonathan to be with him, she hated the idea of his being with someone else.

Edwin followed her over to the other table, unsure whether he would restrain Lynn or make a plea for Helga. Helga looked at Edwin and wondered why she spent so much effort chasing him when Jonathan was always there for her. Jonathan looked at Lynn and Helga and was happy in his belief that one of them might even leave with him.

Now, a situation like this could not possibly get resolved by itself in a way to allow for a neat ending, free from violence and heartbreak and maybe even some spilled wine, without a miracle. However, Edna the waitress, being a creative creature of cleverness, stood on a nearby table and started disrobing to the restaurant's Muzak. Jonathan and Edwin stopped their comments in midsentence and stared at the unexpected floorshow. Helga and Lynn looked at each of the men and then at each other... okay, maybe they snuck a peek at the floorshow too.

But some amazing things started happening. Helga and Lynn left quietly to go to a nearby bar and talk about the things they had in common. Neither one was any good at selecting the men in their lives. As luck would have it, each had a brother who was a perfect match for the other and not long after the introductions were made, all worked well for the new couples in the living-happily-ever-after department.

Edwin started dating Edna and they had a wild relationship. Jonathan was allowed to watch them on alternate Thursdays, which made him happy since that was more excitement than he ever had before.

Noontime Just Looking

Three more strudels were in the pink shop window today than yesterday. Seems that the baker either had more energy in the kitchen or less action at the counter. Didn't matter either way to Fesspot. He was just looking.

Fesspot wandered along his usual noontime path to the drugstore. He perused the magazines but there were no new ones since morning. No matter. He was just looking.

Five minutes later, he was at his usual place at the counter of the diner. He studied the menu as if he had missed a day there in the past two years. He only had the money for a cup of coffee but he didn't plan to buy anything to eat. He was just looking.

The toy store was long gone. He stared in the window anyway. He had never bought anything there when it was open. Apparently, most people had never bought anything there either. The place went under. It was an attractive building though and the store itself was nicely paneled. Real charm. A real good rental deal. But Fesspot was just looking through the window to pass the time. No plans to rent. No real dreams either. Just looking.

There was a cookie shop that had recently opened up next door to the small old theater. Fesspot remembered this and soon was heading southward along the avenue. He still had no money, but he wanted to see what all the fuss was about. On the way, he thought about the strudels, the magazines at the drugstore, the food at the diner, the toys, and the empty paneled store.

He wondered about the cookies when he was severely hit by a blue Subaru. He just wasn't looking.

Abe (If a Pyromaniac and Thief)

He read each night by candlelight the books he took as his. Prices could not deter him from his late-night learning blitz. He lit each page and by the glow he read it as it burned. His eyes would race the spreading flame and this is how he learned.

The Tweezers of Life Somehow Stuck in a Fallen Log

"The tweezers of life are somehow stuck in a fallen log," reported the middle-aged man in the middle-aged suit to a tired police sergeant. "It happened this spring and it could be final."

The sergeant took all of this down as the man rattled off his account of the situation. He had heard all this before. Yesterday, this man's wife had come in with an identical report. A couple of days ago, the man's brother brought in the same story.

Despite not knowing what the tweezers of life were all about, the sergeant sent a couple of his most dependable officers to make a trip out to the fallen log to hopefully put an end to the police station visits by the members of this family.

The two officers came back a couple of hours later and confirmed the reports. The tweezers of life did indeed appear to be stuck in a fallen log.

A bored newspaperman happened to be near the sergeant's desk when the officers returned and the next day's paper featured as its lead story an account of the tweezers of life. The national media picked up the story and soon the whole nation was talking about the strange fate of the tweezers.

A religion was established near the site of the log and people from around the world would come to make the pilgrimage. An amusement park, Six Flags Over the Tweezers, was opened and it flourished.

The man who owned the property around the log became a millionaire. So did his wife and so did his brother. Their fortunes grew as they traveled America, buying worthless land and sticking tweezers into fallen logs.

Seeking a Cure for the Dexters

Sherman tucked in the plaid tie that had sampled his salad. Mr. Hokus didn't seem to notice, since he was busy searching his briefcase for the necessary file. The waitress may or may not have seen Sherman's tie in the salad, but the better-tipped waitresses rarely laugh at the customers.

"It's right here," said a happy Mr. Hokus. "Advice, clues, and addresses. Did you bring the money?"

Sherman handed a thick envelope to Mr. Hokus who put it into his briefcase without inspecting it. Wishing Sherman a quick "Good luck," Mr. Hokus got up to leave and reached into his coat pocket.

"Here is a card that may come in handy," said a serious Mr. Hokus. "They know how to get blue cheese off a plaid tie."

Sherman looked at his tie for a moment. When he looked up, Mr. Hokus was gone. He studied the information in the file. The advice pages seemed to reinforce his ideas about how to solve his problem. They didn't offer much new, however.

The pages of clues were a real baffler to Sherman. Nothing on them seemed to deal with the problem of uninvited guests, and the language they were written in had been extinct for centuries.

The address pages were just that. Addresses only. There was no mention of what lurked at any of the thirty-five addresses. It was about one p.m., and with the sun high in the sky, Sherman decided to take a tour of the city, visiting each address on the list.

He found a pet shop, a shoe store, and a daycare center. He could not understand the importance of any of them. Even so, he kept visiting each address and only found a random assortment of places. He wrote the names of each place in a column. Maybe the first letter of each would provide a clue. Maybe it's like Poe's "Annabelle Lee" where the first letter of each line combines to spell something. Nope. Not a vowel in the bunch.

Sherman found his way home about two a.m. An angry wife greeted him at the door. She held off her angry words when she realized that Sherman was madder than she was. He told her that he had made a purchase that led him on a wild goose chase. He considered taking the gun from the nightstand and paying Mr. Hokus a visit.

"Why are *you* angry?" Sherman inquired of his wife. "I am often late, being the easily distracted type. Aren't you used to me by now?"

"Did you forget our plans tonight?" she asked sternly. "We were supposed to have taken our out-of-town guests to dinner. They got so upset that you didn't show up they packed up and left. And the Dexters are never coming to visit us again!"

Sherman had a sudden smile and he grabbed his wife's hands. He started dancing and his wife, not one to pass up a romantic opportunity, started dancing too. They looked in each other's eyes and considered enjoying the possibilities of the night.

Unfortunately, the stain on Sherman's tie was spotted by his wife and her anger flared up again. She went on and on about his carelessness and he wondered if Mr. Hokus had a file to help him deal with her.

Vaughan's Letter

Vaughan once wrote a letter to the President of the United States. He received a form letter in the mail two weeks later. The letter still hangs on his wall. Vaughan shows it to everybody who walks in front of his house. He drags them into his den and shows them the letter.

The letter is the only thing in the house that hasn't been stolen by strangers.

Suddenly Nero Appeared to Boyd

Suddenly Emperor Nero appeared to Boyd, a man who loved his television. Boyd realized that the second half of the *Get Smart* episode would have to continue without him. He turned off the set.

"Common person," started Nero as he accompanied his words on his fiddle. "I have been transported here through time and space to this room to tell you that there are ways to change your life for the better."

"You have burn marks on your toga," observed Boyd.

"There was a great fire in Rome when I was transported," responded Nero. "I had to leave my job as emperor during a crisis to come here and help you. You had better be receptive to my assistance."

"Should I get a paper and pencil?" inquired Boyd.

"No need for papyrus, my words shall be clear," said Nero. "About your bedwetting problem..."

"I don't wet the bed!" responded Boyd quickly.

"Aren't you Hiram the Majestic?" asked a puzzled Nero.

"My name is Boyd."

Nero looked out the window to see a lit concrete walkway dividing a carefully mowed lawn between trimmed hedges. There were no waves, no water. A mistake had clearly been made.

"How far are we from the Atlantic Ocean?" inquired Nero.

Boyd took down the globe that was on the top of his bookshelf and showed him the distance between Nebraska and the Atlantic. Nero understood that a major error had occurred. He continued to look at the globe carefully as if looking for something.

"I guess the world looks quite different than it did in your day," said Boyd as Nero's concern grew. "Rome is now Italy and it's very beautiful there now."

Boyd hoped to console the famous emperor by bringing out his photo album from his trip through Italy a few years before. This had little success. Nero's problem was not about what had happened to Rome.

"Nothing is named after me!" shouted Nero as he handed the globe back to Boyd. He appeared to be a defeated man.

"I am the most powerful person in the world, at least when I return to my empire, and there is nothing on your globe to indicate that I even existed. Surely, there is a city, an island, a country – something named after me."

"I'm afraid that you weren't considered a very good ruler," said Boyd as tactfully as possible. "Perhaps setting fire to Rome was not a good move. Of course, I may not know that much about how nations should be administered."

Boyd was thankful that Nero was not accompanied by any of his soldiers. He scratched his head and appreciated that it was still attached to the rest of him. Nero, however, looked too sad to have even considered such an order.

"You may be right, Boyd," said a somber Nero. "My life must not have been appreciated by the gods. I have been forgotten by your globe and my fate is to be transported through time to assist people with bladder problems. I know that it's too late to change my life for the better, so may I borrow some sheet music? It's too bright outside my palace to sleep."

Nero pointed to the piano bench by the window. Boyd opened it and pulled out some sheet music for a few Dylan tunes. Nero looked content as he held them tightly before suddenly disappearing.

Boyd was happy as he realized that there were still a good six or seven minutes left of *Get Smart*. He settled back in his easy chair. He was happy also that the powers that be had allowed him to be free from bladder problems.

Carbon, Yes, It Was Carbon

Carbon, yes, it was carbon.

There really should not have been any doubt, what with all the problems it created, but she said it was coal. I always thought that charcoal was coal, and that coal was carbon.

If you looked in her eyes when I did, you would have been unsure about anything they told you in high school. As it happened, I spoke up anyway.

When things are ready to fall apart, anything can become a battleground, even carbon. Or rather, even whatever charcoal really is. I still haven't bothered to look it up. It doesn't matter now.

Imagine discussing all that after a night of watching a great play. I forgot the name of it, but it was by Breck, or Brecht, or Brett. I don't remember everything I've seen, but I do remember one thing for sure.

Carbon, yes, it was carbon.

Ask Wisconsin/The Oncoming Bureau of Longitudes

"We have Wisconsin on the phone."
"Madison?"
"No, not Madison."

Four loopy edging stones cascaded into the Oncoming Bureau of Longitudes while we the paupers stood and applauded, muskets encouraging our display of enthusiasm.

"Sheboygan?"
"No, not Sheboygan either."

"This sort of cascade is quite rare in this radius," said the elder, a sincere and filibustering man of cheese.

"Milwaukee perhaps?"
"No, sorry."

Walking wildly among the blue spots, the suntan kind etched across the torpedoed horizon. "This was once all calves and helmets," he lamented.

"Eau Claire?"
"No. Wrong again."

Eking a mass existence from beside the bedrock plateau nearest the butler tray, he slowly cut the red wax. It easily parted.

"Green Bay? It has to be Green Bay."
"No."

We the paupers stared at the crackers that had been placed on the monkey plates before us. Ours was the wind. Ours was the sun and the rain. Ours were the clouds shaped like otters. These barefaced crackers, however, cheesed us off.

"Appleton?"
"Wrong again."

The elders waved through high windows of attitude as they munched on the palest yellow of cheeses. Their crackers were full. Their crackers were happy. Their crackers runneth over with sweet fromage.

We threw the loopy edging stones far into the field where the elders never trod, where approaching muskets would be grabbed by monkeys eager to shoot at distant plates and sad crackers. We lamented the day's direction. We needed some closure. We needed some victory. We needed to applaud in sincerity.

"Racine?"
"Yes."

"Hooray!" we the paupers shouted as our thrown hats descended back down to us. The elders waved again to us from their lofty tables high in the latitudes. They would take their bows for whatever occurred, even before they learned what we had celebrated.

Rabid at Best (Episode III)

She was rabid at best as she strolled the arena and heard from the prophets of what was to be. She never did turn when her usher had hovered, so a decade had passed and then half of another.

She bumped her dear usher with handfuls of papers. The leopard and lion were missing or dead. They chatted, both planted in new decade matters and slowly reacted to what each had said.

"Dear usher," she said as she froze her ex-lover. "Dear usher," she said as she looked in his eyes. "Intensity leads to a prison of heartbeats. Intensity leads to a grasping of straws. A lover in bed is a reason for living. A lover long gone is a loser with flaws."

The usher just smiled as he offered the wisdom of time and of life as it leads from a lover. No music was blaring, no penguins were staring, the usher was happy to find a back cover.

She was rabid at best, but most likely just floating on long-distant dreams that had sputtered from will. She had papers to carry away from the prophets, and away from the hedges, forever and still.

Seven or Eight Moderately Sized Amphibians

Seven or eight moderately sized amphibians gathered by the side of a large pond named Edgar to decide the true reason for their existence. One of them, a green one with bumps, wanted to use the gathering as a forum for his lifetime of observations. He took out a hundred or so index cards that had his notes and he cleared his throat.

He spoke for a good hour before flipping to his second index card. Although amphibians are not known for their mathematical abilities because of their relative brain size, the remaining six or seven moderately sized amphibians multiplied the ninety-nine unused index cards by one hour each and came up with a total of a heck of a lot. One of them theorized that it might even be a *whole* heck of a lot of time before the green one with bumps concluded.

They decided that for the good of the majority, they would stop the speaker by devouring him. So they did. Their problem was solved and they dispersed to independently contemplate the level of wisdom of their actions.

While each was snuggled within the relative safety of his respective hole in the ground or under the bushes or underwater, a group of high schoolers armed with nets gathered them all up and took them to a garage where they were deposited in a wooden cage.

They all felt they had been arrested for their deeds. It was only after a great deal of time had elapsed that they understood by the conversation of the students that they had not been brought to the garage because of what they had done to the green one with bumps. The high schoolers seemed unaware that the group of amphibians had so recently been one more. The students made no mention of a crime.

"Perhaps we deserve whatever lies in store for us," theorized a yellowish moderately sized amphibian. "We did wrong and now we are to be punished. Yes, it may be true that our captors don't know what we did, but we did wrong and now we are about to pay for it. Justice is justice."

The other five or six moderately sized amphibians were silent as the yellowish one explained to them using logic, parables, and semaphore. They were still as he went on about karma and "he who lives by killing moderately sized amphibians shall die as a moderately sized amphibian."

After two hours, the five or six bored and desperate moderately sized amphibians pounced on the yellowish one and devoured him. In their state of emotional energy, they also managed to bite their way through their wooden cage and escape. They ran, as well as they were capable of, back to the pond named Edgar and hid in new hiding places.

The high schoolers came looking for them but while en route to the pond saw a carload of babes and lost interest in the five or six escaping moderately sized amphibians. The small but vicious population of Pond Edgar was safe.

One of them, a grayish-green one, thought that perhaps since they weren't to be punished that, based on the logic put forth by the late yellowish one, they had committed no crime. However, he was too afraid to share his reasoning with his fellow moderately sized amphibians.

Another had an endless stream of questions on right and wrong, but he too was too afraid to take up the time of his fellow vicious pals and risk their wrath. All had questions or ideas, but their thoughts would be kept inside for their protection.

The next day, the next week, and forevermore, the five or six surviving moderately sized amphibians remained silent. They never communicated with each other for fear of speaking too long and being devoured.

One by one, they realized that being unable to communicate with their fellow moderately sized amphibians was the punishment for their deeds. They wondered which of the others had made the same realization, but they were unable to find out for sure.

They all died lonely deaths after living out lonely lives.

Moral: Every crime carries its own punishment.

My Lady's Best Crackers

She must have been anxious to impress. These weren't your typical saltines. These were something she probably bought at Trader Joe's. She smiled at me and I laughed out some of the crackers across the carpet.

I was embarrassed. She brought out some champagne. Good quality stuff here too. Actually, I was so lost in her smile it could have been Windex.

She started a fire, which regrettably took place in the toaster. She was embarrassed. I poured her some champagne.

We talked about love and peace and friendship and sadnesses past. We studied the fireglow in each other's eyes. We wrestled on the carpet. I asked her for more crackers.

We ended a sad year in style.

Lasagna Solutions (A Radio Play)

ANNOUNCER: George is lying on his couch in his living room, in his home, in the middle of a warm afternoon in Anytown, USA, a place that makes a fortune from licensing out its name to movies, books, and plays. Claire is his neighbor. She, like George, lives alone for reasons that will soon become apparent. She is approximately his age, at that time in their lives when birthdays are best forgotten.

CLAIRE: Hello, George! I was worried I would be disturbing you at home. But then I thought, "Hey, good old George told me not to be a stranger." You did say that once, George. It was about eleven years, three months, two weeks, and five days ago, but you said it. I have it on tape. So I picked now not to be a stranger.

GEORGE: How did you get in? I thought I locked the door. Wait, I double-checked right before my nap. I did lock the door.

CLAIRE: Well yes, George, you locked the door. But thoughtful me, always prepared. I should have been a Cub Scout or a Boy Scout but they said, "No you can't be a Cub Scout or a Boy Scout, because you are a girl and girls have to be Girl Scouts or Bluebirds or Brownies or Campfire Girls or Granddaughters of the American..."

GEORGE: Claire. How did you get in?

CLAIRE: Oh, I had a brick in my purse. Don't forget to sweep up the glass. Pesky stuff, broken glass. Yes indeed. Would you like some coffee, George? You look distressed. Make me some too while you're at it. Can you bake us some lasagna too? You look hungry and it worries me to see you that way. Nothing quite like Italian cuisine to put a sparkle in your eyes and give you a bushy tail, if you're inclined to look.

GEORGE: Leave, Claire.

CLAIRE: Oh, George. There you go again. Always joking. I remember the time you threw the party and all of your friends were there. And when I showed up, you kidder you, you told me that I wasn't invited. I know you, George. My invitation must have just gotten lost in the mail.

GEORGE: Leave, Claire.

CLAIRE: But I was such a hit at your party! Everyone was gathered around me. They were all hanging on my every word. I was so glad I'd been going through your mail every morning. They all wanted to hear all about your operation and, as luck would have it, I had your bill in my purse to quote from. Are you sitting on a soft pillow now, George? I certainly hope so. I worry about you. And your friends wanted to hear all about those magazines the mailman brings you. Tsk, tsk, tsk. Those men in the pictures forgot their swim trunks, didn't they?

GEORGE: Okay, Claire. You sit there and I'll get some coffee.

ANNOUNCER: George leaves the room and Claire picks up a stack of his mail. As she opens each envelope, she is distracted by strange noises coming from her house next door. After about ten minutes, George returns with a cup of coffee for himself only.

CLAIRE: Where's my coffee, George? You kidder you.

GEORGE: I am sorry, Claire, but you only had enough for one cup and you told me I needed it.

CLAIRE: I only had enough? George, did you get into my kitchen? I thought I locked the back door.

GEORGE: Well you did, Claire, so I got in through the front.

CLAIRE: But George, I locked that too.

GEORGE: Right again, Claire. Fortunately, I was prepared. I was a Cub Scout and a Boy Scout and an Eagle Scout and an Indian Guide and a Young Republican and...

CLAIRE: How did you get in, George?

GEORGE: I drove my camper through your front door. Took a left... no, that was a right. Well, it should have been a right. I made the left first. You had a beautiful bedroom. I had no idea that a waterbed held that much water... But I finally righted my course and took the dining room route to your kitchen. Your dogs were barking loudly as they chased me. Strange though, their barking stopped shortly after I backed out of your kitchen and went over some bumps. Care for a sip?

CLAIRE: George, you beast, I am leaving. Yes, I am.

ANNOUNCER: Claire leaves and George pictures a plate of lasagna as the solution to his problems. He is very depressed so he decides to end his life by ordering lasagna at a coffee shop. He lists his next of kin on a piece of paper that he folds and places in his pocket before he leaves. Arriving at the local Denny's, George finds a seat in the only chair available. It is at a table in the back and there is a sign on it reading "This Table for Philosophical Discussion Only." A man already seated at the table and wearing a brown suit, looks over some notes in great anticipation of a conversation. His name is Fred, but it could just as easily have been Max or Genghis the Zebra Skinner, since George never calls him by name.

FRED: Nothing ends but everything begins!

GEORGE: What?!?

FRED: Nothing ends but everything begins! Profound isn't it. Sorta makes me want to grow a beard.

GEORGE: What are you talking about?

FRED: The sign. Didn't you read the sign?

GEORGE: Yes, I saw it, but it's only a sign.

FRED: Only a sign?!?

GEORGE: Yes, looks like only a sign to me.

FRED: How can you say that?

GEORGE: In English, French, Latin, and, if you'll pardon my grammar, in German, too.

FRED: You're putting me on now, aren't you? You can't refer to a sign as only a sign. What you call "only a sign" is a statement of proposed reality. A "Keep Off the Grass" sign can create a condition where nobody walks on the grass. There was a sign down the street saying "Future Site of Broadway Department Store" and darn my socks if there wasn't one there nine months later. Now consider the deeper meanings of this sign as I begin our philosophical discussion again... Nothing ends but everything begins!

GEORGE: I think I'll end this conversation by leaving and prove you wrong.

FRED: I'll still be talking so I will have been right again. I'm good at this. I will grow a beard. Now you disagree with me and we'll go from there.

GEORGE: I disagree with you. I'm leaving.

FRED: You can't do that. I have a grenade in my coat pocket and I can hit anything in a three-hundred-foot range. A real talent but perhaps not one I should have included on my résumé. I'm unemployed and depressed and I don't even get mail from Ed McMahon... Now argue with me properly or else!

GEORGE: Okay, I need to ask you a few questions to build my case. When you said, "Nothing ends but everything begins" did you mean that for all concepts also?

FRED: Yes... Hey, this is good. Have you done this before?

GEORGE: Do you accept the concept of absence?

FRED: Run that by me again.

GEORGE: I mean, can you appreciate the absence of something?

FRED: Besides my ex-wife? Yes, I suppose so. Absence is a concept.

GEORGE: Well, since absence ends when something begins and absence is a concept, and a concept is a thing, then something ends and your argument, by modus ponens, modus tollens, and modus tollendo ponens, bites the big one.

FRED: You win. Congratulations!

ANNOUNCER: George's prize is his lasagna, which was remarkably better than he expected since he lived to tell about it. He lived a long and prosperous life and enjoyed watching television at night, after finally subscribing to cable. George introduced Fred to Claire and they soon got married and moved to a small town where they eventually became the only residents. The end.

Edgar and the Trade School

"Name," stated the well-perfumed woman behind the counter, without even a glance at the person who had just entered the trade school office.

"Yes," responded a daydreaming Edgar. After a pause during which he realized his response needed embellishing, he added, "Edgar. Edgar Sullivan."

"What courses are you interested in?" asked the woman.

"Actually, I don't really know what your school offers," responded Edgar.

This response was worth a quick glance from the woman. She told him to be seated, and he walked to the chair within reach of the most interesting magazines. She picked up the phone and pushed a button. Edgar heard her softly say something about a "live one."

A man in his early fifties who probably received his tie as a gift from his wife came out to greet Edgar as he was midway through an article about Elvis' ghost appearing in a laundromat to wash sheets. Edgar was escorted through a maze of rooms and hallways to an office. The man, who introduced himself as Max, sat behind a desk. Edgar looked at the woman in the photograph on his desk and decided she had bought him his tie.

"Did you bring your checkbook?" asked Max.

"Yes, but I thought I would look this place over first," answered Edgar.

"Did you like what you saw when we walked to this office?" asked Max.

"It was quite a walk," said Edgar. "All those twists and turns. I don't think I would ever be able to find my way back."

"You're very intelligent, Edgar," said Max. "That's good. Please make out a check to this school for five hundred dollars so we can get you started with some classes."

"I haven't decided if I'm attending your school yet," Edgar said with a touch of anger at Max's pushiness.

"I'll be back when you've signed your check," said Max as he bolted out of the office before a startled Edgar could follow him.

Edgar remained in his chair and thought to himself that Max would be back. "This is like one of those job interviews where the person hiring does something strange just to see how a prospective employee responds," he thought to himself.

Edgar recalled the man at the toaster plant who pretended to have a heart attack, and the woman at the Buick polishing company who did some sophisticated Taekwondo moves on her desk. Edgar decided that Max would be back. He was glad that he had brought the magazine with the article about Elvis' ghost.

After learning all there was about the sighting in the laundromat, Edgar's attention was focused on other matters. He read about Elizabeth Taylor's secret marriage to Ho Chi Minh, Phil Donahue's battle with occasionally keeping library books beyond their due date, and why people who get shot out of cannons are more at risk of early deaths than those who live to be ninety.

Three hours later, Edgar was growing impatient. Max had not returned and Edgar was eager to share his wealth of newly read information with anyone sitting close enough to him at Gulliver's Pub. He was angry to have fallen for the sales pitch of this trade school. They had great commercials and they were always on at the most effective times, when the audience was the most receptive to whatever was said. Their jingle was catchy too. Edgar had seen their commercial during *Geraldo* when his demand for credibility was at its lowest level.

Afternoon television seems to consistently remind those watching that they are desperate for something to do with their days. Edgar, having been unemployed for some time, was indeed desperate.

Edgar knew that the economy was doing very well and he was grateful for the media that made him aware that somewhere money was indeed plentiful. He had believed that things were tough all over and after asking his friends, his contention had been strengthened. Now that he was informed otherwise, he wanted his fair share.

He scanned the classifieds every day. He followed up by calling about twenty jobs each day before finally settling down with *Oprah* and *Geraldo*. Each call met with a different reason for failure.

Edgar's inexperience in public relations cost him the job as a security guard. Because he knew nothing about repairing the latest Zoltar X-318 Digital System, he lost out on the job in the strawberry patch. His inability to recall the specifics of the Atomic Energy Act caused him to be passed by as an Anaheim Stadium vendor. The shoeshine stand owner hung up after Edgar could not name the starting infield of the 1926 St. Louis Browns.

Edgar called the number in the commercial that promised to teach him the necessary skills to get a job. A representative came out to see him a few days later and convinced him to visit the office. She had not told him much about the school itself, and Edgar thought it strange that she had no brochures or catalogues to give him. She did, however, look good in her sequined dress and that appealed to Edgar's taste in staring.

He agreed to an appointment at the school offices the next day, but he didn't show up. Someone called him in an attempt to reschedule for the following week. Edgar, however, had more resolve in the absence of the sequined representative.

Every day for three weeks, someone called Edgar from the trade school. Every day he received several letters from them. After tiring of slamming his front door in the faces of their representatives, he stopped responding to his doorbell. One day during *Geraldo*, their commercial featured the words, "Edgar Sullivan, are you going to show up or what?" above their phone number.

It was a phone call on the following Wednesday that finally convinced Edgar to reschedule his visit. Perhaps their argument was sinking in or perhaps it was the way his girlfriend pleaded with him over the phone to "do whatever they want" because "the guy's got a gun," but either way Edgar scheduled an appointment.

Edgar awoke from his daydream in Max's office and decided to attempt to find his way through the maze of hallways to the front door. He walked slowly out of the office trying to remember everything he saw in case he had to return. The hallways, however, were empty. No furniture. Nothing on the walls. Nothing to remember.

Edgar reached into his pants pocket and opened a plastic container of Tic Tacs. Dropping them every few feet, he wandered the hallways for about an hour.

He saw the cow's skeletal remains at the same time he ran out of Tic Tacs. The two factors combined to inspire his return to the office. He gave up and wrote the check for five hundred dollars. The moment he placed it on Max's desk, Max returned.

"Just what does this entitle me to?" asked Edgar.

"You get five six-week courses, Edgar," responded Max. "Believe me, you will be more valuable in the job market once you have completed the courses. The first will show you how to be a medical professional in the use of leeches. You will then have a course in navigation."

"I love the sea," commented Edgar, making the best of the situation as Max examined his check.

"That course is unique because it teaches the navigating techniques needed in sailing the flat Earth and avoiding those pesky edges," added Max. "The third course teaches skills in loading muskets."

"Muskets?" asked Edgar. "Like they used in the Revolutionary War?"

"Yes!" responded an enthusiastic Max. "I must make a note to get you a seat in the advanced class. The fourth class is on alchemy."

"Alchemy?" asked Edgar. "Will I be able to turn common metals into gold?"

"Well, that hasn't been accomplished yet," said Max. "But so much has been learned in this field that the breakthrough could come at any time. Our teachers are all researchers. The fifth class is entitled 'How to Profit from Serfdom.' You will learn how to make the most of serfdom, whether you decide to become a serf or simply want to invest in the system."

"That's it! That's the final straw!" shouted Edgar. "Leeches, flat Earth navigation, muskets, alchemy, and serfdom? All these are from centuries ago. How will they help me find any job?"

"Well, our staff has done a great deal of research in this area," replied a calm Max. "They have shown me the numbers and it seems that there were far fewer people unemployed when these skills were studied and practiced."

Max brought out a report and handed it to Edgar. Impressed by the numbers and graphics in the report, Edgar did not think about pointing out that the world population was significantly smaller so long ago, and that therefore unemployment was much less.

Edgar turned out to be quite happy with the trade school and attended every session. His education qualified him for a government job, where he works to this day.

Kevin the Weasel and the Goodtime Lunch Brigade

It was about that time again as young Melvin sat not two feet from the Magnavox and opened his Kevin the Weasel lunchbox. All was in readiness: the bologna sandwich, the Fritos, the three Chips Ahoys... and the thermos containing cherry punch.

The theme song filled the room:

Dudes and dudettes relaxing in the shade
Indoors or outdoors, you've really got it made
Join us and we'll eat together, more fun than if you played
It's Kevin the Weasel and the Goodtime Lunch Brigade.

Melvin sang along, occasionally getting a word correct. He swayed. He smiled. He awaited the weasel.

The weasel made his usual exciting entrance and promised cartoons and visits from the usual characters: Osmond the Lizard, Claire the Toaster, and Winston the Hologram.

Melvin ate his lunch. All of it!

He sat for half an hour with his television pals. Then it was over... and Melvin went into the backyard to finish building Melvinville in the sandbox.

There is nothing profound in this story. No allegories to deeper meanings in life. Nope, not this time. *Kevin the Weasel and the Goodtime Lunch Brigade* occupies half an hour five times a week in the life of young Melvin. Other than getting him to finish his lunch, it doesn't have much to do with the realities of the life he will come to know.

He won't even remember the day he outgrows it.

The Enron Cup

"My landlord is poisoning Christians with Liquid Gold," Delia said as she stared at my eyebrows. I looked into the Enron mug I held that was half-filled with the coffee she made while I wasn't watching her.

"It's a cup, not a mug," she explained. "And no, you didn't spill any on your shirt. And yes, you turned off the radio in your bathroom before you drove over."

I was silent. She was in my mind again. I didn't have to say a word for her to hear me. I thought she was crazy and I knew I couldn't hide that thought from her for long. My only chance was to ponder insanity as a good thing... or maybe change the subject.

"Where did you get this Enron cup?" I asked.

"I bought it on eBay," she replied. "I like the idea of celebrating the darker part of the human character."

"And she can read my thoughts," I thought to myself.

"Yes, I can read your thoughts," she said.

I wanted to ask her something else, not that I had to say it aloud. I just hoped that if I focused on my words, maybe I would keep from thinking anything that might set her off. Alas, with this pressure, I sat nervously with a hundred thoughts running through my head.

"Do you want the Enron cup?" she asked.

I said yes and for a moment I was happy. I hadn't thought about wanting the cup for myself and yet she ignored whatever I was thinking to ask this. This seemed like an act of kindness. There was another pause.

"My ex-husband will fall out of a window this afternoon," she said, breaking the silence.

"Is this a good thing?" I asked.

"Yes, very," she said coldly. "He has been hypnotizing students to become snipers on campus."

"I didn't hear about any snipings lately," I replied as politely as possible.

"They haven't started yet. He has planned it all to all happen on the same day, our wedding anniversary."

"How do you know this?" I asked.

"The same way I know what you are thinking."

There was a longer pause this time. She got up and went into another room. I was frozen in place.

"This is for you," she said and handed me a box. "Go put it in your car with the Enron cup."

"Should I do it now?"

"Yes! Now! Go!" she shouted.

I ran to my car. I placed the box and cup on the passenger side floor. I froze in place. I couldn't move. I felt no panic at all though. I closed my eyes and felt at peace.

When I opened my eyes, I was home in my easy chair. It was evening. The news was on but the sound was off. The news showed a photograph of Delia's ex-husband and I could see that he died just the way she said he would. They then showed film of Delia's house and I knew inside that she was dead also. The scene shifted to an older man with a large ring of keys on his belt lying on the ground with cans of Liquid Gold scattered all around him.

"What's next?" I wondered aloud.

"We're here, so don't say anything incriminating," said Wilhelmina and Carlos in unison from the couch that I hadn't yet looked at since I awoke.

"We don't want to know anything about you of consequence," continued Wilhelmina solo. "Hey, this is a nifty cup!"

"Yes, it is," I replied. "Delia gave it to me. She liked the idea of owning a souvenir from Enron. Hmmmm... I guess I didn't dream that part. I was there today... or yesterday. What day is it?"

"Today? Why it's St. Martyr of the Terrible Inconvenience Day," replied Carlos as he inspected the Enron cup.

"St. Martyr of the Terrible Inconvenience Day?" I said slowly. "Then the spirits have done all their work in a matter of hours."

"What spirits?" inquired Wilhelmina.

"Well, I am not sure, but I know that it is only a matter of time before the authorities fish your goat, Whiskers, out of the Buchanans' whisky grotto."

"Yikes!" shouted Carlos, and he and Wilhelmina were quickly gone to attempt some serious future averting.

I was alone. This was good. My distracters were all gone. Delia was dead and I knew I would never see Carlos or Wilhelmina again. I was finally back to being my old self. The television was still on. The Enron cup was on my coffee table.

Things may have disintegrated into bizarre randomness in my life, but until the day of the snipings, I knew that all would be right in my world. I smiled as I sorted through the money, coupons, and instructions in the box that Delia had given me.

Welcoming the Dark Blue Arms of Springtime

A police car drove down Anna Maria's avenue without even slowing down. The officer riding shotgun only gave a passing glance to the banner that hung over her porch steps. His mind was on the problem at the airport.

Anna Maria peeked through the lacy curtains of her living room window. She consoled herself with a Diet Coke as she slumped into her favorite chair. She had come so close this time. She stared at the man in the framed photograph above the fireplace. She thought again about how and why he made his escape.

The room shook but it wasn't any big deal. It was only the train that crossed her avenue a block away every afternoon at about this time. Anna Maria's eyes lit up with the sudden inspiration to try again tomorrow.

Her next morning was uneventful. She tried again to reach the supervisor at her last job. He hadn't returned her calls for a couple of weeks and she hoped that the company was finally through its problems and was ready for her to come back to work. She wondered if any of the others who had left when she did were back yet.

She found her old box of love letters just after noon. She read the most recent ones, the ones she received about a year and a half before. She put the box away and washed her face. She spent some time quietly staring into the man's eyes in the photograph above her fireplace as her mind replayed his promises.

"He will be back," she thought to herself. "He said he would be back."

She fell asleep in her chair. Her phone didn't ring so she slept undisturbed. The train's rumbling is what woke her. She was upset when she realized she had missed an opportunity but she smiled when she looked at her watch. The train was once again right on time.

Nothing notable happened to Anna Maria until the next afternoon. She had thought about the man in the picture a few times and another few moments were spent running to the front window to see if anyone was coming up the walkway.

That afternoon, she looked at her watch and made her phone call. She spoke slowly and deliberately and the train arrived right on time. The train loudly passed before she hung up.

The banner was still in place as Anna Maria stood in her front yard and read it aloud, "Welcome to the Dark Blue Arms of Springtime." She turned when a car passed but it wasn't the right one. A police car finally did drive by and she stared at it until it passed. The officers looked at her and were tempted to stop, but they had more important business. The evening's basketball game might have to be postponed. At the same moment they drove by Anna Maria, some of their fellow men in blue were already searching the arena.

Anna Maria went back inside and turned on the news. There was no mention of the sound of a train in the call. She sat in her favorite chair and closed her eyes. How she wished that the chair would swallow her up. How she longed to disappear slowly into something warm.

The blue arms would never come for her. That afternoon was her last try. She took down the banner and spent the evening staring at the photograph.

Eventually, her supervisor would call and she would be back at her old desk. Eventually, the man in the photograph would come back for her, but it would be long after his photograph was thrown away and Anna Maria found someone else to lean on.

Escapes are always more complicated than expected.

Pigtails

Nancy was chosen as Little Miss Pigtails at her nursery school pageant. She was chosen Miss Pigtails at her junior high school pageant. She was chosen Ms. Pigtails at her high school pageant.

Nancy went to some silly schools.

Princes Are Like Otters Because...

"It's all gone, Edgewater," said Grandma Hartfield in the general direction of the zincshield, "the wear and the tear and the tango. Now it's this and all of it is this."

Edgewater handed her the rubber pork chop and she hit the poster head on.

"You have been good and faithful," she continued, "a marble among men of your stature. Now comes the time for contraction, for falling, for things washed by scenery."

Edgewater surveyed that scenery. There was blue tile everywhere. On the floor, on the walls, on the ceiling. He reached for the rubber pork chop and once again handed it to her. She took aim and the ceramic water tower was history. A blue light shone through the half-closed blinds.

"Princes are just like otters," she said. She grimaced in deep thought to complete the bit of wisdom she was trying to leave behind. After three minutes, Edgewater broke the silence.

"Who will get the zincshield?" he asked. He immediately wondered about the propriety of his question. Grandma Hartfield was still breathing, living, and, to some degree thinking.

"The zincshield is still for the ages of time spent pondering," she said slowly and deliberately. "Make me a list of your favorite people and five vegetables and we'll draw squiglets."

Edgewater soon had everything in readiness as he looked at his watch and waited for Grandma Hartfield to make her move. She looked at him the instant he looked at his watch.

"Daisy can wait," she said. Edgewater wondered who Daisy was.

"Daisy's dead, you know," she said. "She told me that she died a week ago. Princes are like otters..."

There was another long silence, which was only broken when Grandma Hartfield commented on Edgewater's squiglet.

"This could have been more thoroughly drawn by a veritable army," she said and Edgewater could only nod. "Perhaps I shall find that army and give them the zincshield."

Edgewater believed that the afternoon and early evening had been wasted until he looked between the blinds to learn the source of the blue light. The zincshield had slipped from its hinges and through it the moonlight had been amplified and colored before it entered the room.

"Princes really are like otters," Grandma Hartfield insisted. "Maybe because Daisy is dead, I'm not sure."

Daisy entered the room and Grandma Hartfield considered alternate theories. Daisy escorted Grandma Hartfield to the bed and brought her a stuffed otter.

"This is my pal Prince," said Grandma Hartfield, who then turned to her stuffed colleague. "Prince, these are two people who are not otters."

Edgewater and Daisy each took a stuffed otter paw and shook it gently as a greeting. Grandma Hartfield fell asleep. When it was clear to all that she would never wake up, Edgewater worried about who would get the zincshield.

"She never did announce who would get the zincshield," he said to Daisy.

"You really wouldn't want it," Daisy responded. "That's why she gave you me instead."

"Can she do that?" Edgewater inquired.

"I didn't think so until I saw it in writing," she responded.

Edgewater decided to make full use of the bequeathment and while they were on the tile floor the room shook. "I'm usually not this good," Edgewater thought to himself. He was right. The ground shook because troops had entered the room.

"I'm Captain Slosher and we're the Veritable Army," said the one with the most decorations on his uniform. "We're here for the zincshield. Here are my papers."

Both Edgewater and Daisy were impressed with the squiglet on Captain Slosher's papers. After the Veritable Army had left the room to dismantle and take the zincshield, Daisy and Edgewater decided to go invest in a manual and discuss the meaning of life over SpaghettiOs.

That night, all was clear to Daisy. She did her best to explain it to Edgewater as he considered the possibilities of page 35.

"You didn't get the zincshield, but you got me," she said and turned to find Edgewater on his head with his left leg over the couch and his right leg in midair. He looked at her, landed on the floor, and returned to where he had been sitting on the couch.

"You can't get what you think you want most out of life," Daisy continued. "You can get something resembling love, however, if you can somehow get it in writing."

Edgewater nodded and considered page 36. Daisy went into the kitchen to check on the progress of the SpaghettiOs.

The Ox Died

The ox died. It's really important that you keep that in mind or no good will come of the story that I am about to relate to you. It happened on a sunny November day out in a field when there was work to be done, fields to plow, lots of things like that.

Florence was at the receiving end of the message I sent over the intercom. She could have been wearing a green dress or a red suit. I know not the color that highlighted her features. She took down the message word-for-word, "The ox died."

The ox was no more. It breatheth not. Florence relayed the message. Nobody seemed interested. I have lost interest myself in the years that have come and gone since the occurrence in the field that November day while the birds chirped and the trees did whatever trees do in the course of a day.

I am now in the plumbing business. Florence ran off with somebody in a dark suit. The ox died that November day so he hasn't done much since.

But I remember that November day and how I carefully chose my words and gave that message. I didn't think about the look on Florence's face or what she was wearing when I told her what I knew to be the truth:

The ox died.

The Lancaster Set

"Did you mention the vent flu sediment in your answer for number six?"

"The what?"

"Vent flu sediment. It was the cat's pajamas for the Lancaster Set."

"Question four, you mean?"

"Yeah, that could have been it. I lost track of time in there."

"Time has that habit. What was the deal with the Norwegian weasel? Should he be given the camellia or the Wisconsin vacation?"

"I think he was killed in the kiting mishap. At least that's what I wrote, but I write sloppy on purpose."

"How many dents were there in the multiple choice?"

"Seven or eight. The plaza sandbox tripped me up."

"Goodness in sandals! I only put three!"

"Don't worry. It's a religious holiday. That's worth something."

"Was it Harding's ghetto blaster or the zinc display that put an end to tires as we know them?"

"Don't tell me you actually got to the bonus question!"

"I always start from the side and work across. Numbers and landmarks are less of a hassle that way."

"Well, here is where I need to turn left to progress through my day. Thank you for telling me about this. You were right. This was a lot of fun."

"There's another final tomorrow morning in King Hall 773."

"Can you loan me a blue book for it?"

"Sure, I have plenty. The test begins at ten."

"What's the subject?"

"I find this is more fun when we don't really know."

"Another good answer. See you tomorrow."

The Lori Lies

"You know, if you knew the whole picture you wouldn't write about the small pieces that you know about," said Vito, who sat behind his writing samples at the south end of an outdoor table. "When the walls that keep us from understanding what it's really all about start to fall, well, you'll look rather foolish with your preoccupations with the little you know."

Lori, who maintained the conversational responsibilities of the north end of the outdoor table, paused to consider whatever wisdom might have been in Vito's words. Vito, realizing his theoretical pontifications may have overextended his mental abilities at the expense of Lori's feelings, immediately backtracked.

"All of us writers are going to look rather foolish," Vito said as he stared into Lori's eyes, "but there's something noble in our efforts nonetheless. Something Don Quixotelike."

Lori seemed to be buying Vito's latest words. Vito offered to buy her a drink: an iced tea, a beer, water. Lori declined, instead looking at one of Vito's stories. She paused momentarily to measure his words against absolute truths. Or at least she seemed to.

Vito and Lori were soon walking along the hard black surface of the parking lot. Inspired by the possibilities, Vito imagined it was a field of black grass. He was tempted to pick up an inviting piece of asphalt and toss it beyond a Chrysler. He looked at Lori instead. She picked up the piece and threw it farther than Vito would have. He was impressed.

"We are all writers, Lori," started Vito. "As long as the black manmade rocks clear the Chryslers in our lives, does it truly matter whose hands are black afterward?"

Lori looked at him and held his hand. He thought that they had connected on a deep level. He wouldn't notice the blackness on his own hand until much later. Even then, he wouldn't really know if she took his hand as a joke or as a response to his question.

For months, he would ponder whether or not she was sincere or if it was all just a game to her. When he finally reached a conclusion, it would be wrong. Vito could bluff a connection with almost anyone but he would one day realize that he simply wasn't in her league.

Edging into Soda Junction (Episode One)

Edging into Soda Junction were the Twoboats, Iris and Keystrokes, and their misinformed poodle, Manta Ray. A local, seated on the bench under the shade of the "Who Goes There?" sign, stared, gazed, and watched them shuffle along the far side of the dirt road.

"He seems to be looking at us, Keystrokes," said a concerned Iris. "Perhaps we should detach the balloons from our entourage."

Keystrokes looked up at the balloons. They were impressive and a key component of who he imagined himself to be. One was a giant otter, another was a rounded Buick. His favorite, however, was the large Ethel Mertz balloon he bought at the Plaid Forest in 1973. He couldn't see most of it though. The Tommy Toaster balloon and the "Hooray for Paraphernalia" balloons blocked his view.

"Buzz buzz," said Manta Ray. Iris simply shook her head.

"We're running out of towns to edge into," she said sadly.

Keystrokes agreed by keeping quiet. He knew her next words. They were unavoidable. He cringed slightly.

"It's either the balloons or me!" she said. "Manta Ray, I happen to be neutral about. It's your call on that issue."

"Buzz buzz?" inquired Manta Ray.

"Yes, she was talking about you," responded Keystrokes, hoping to scare up an ally.

"Where are you folks headed?!" shouted the man under the sign.

"We're not sure!" Keystrokes shouted back. "Is there a place in town with a bed, a doghouse, and a place to hitch these balloons, preferably someplace with a lot of porcelain?"

"Well, there's the Inn de Plume, but they don't have any doghouses." the man replied. "The Happy Hotel has doghouses but no porcelain. The Motel '98 has no beds. It's actually a huge mural on a wall by a traveling artist who was looking to make some beer money."

The Twoboats thanked the man as they walked into town anyway. They were prepared to take on any challenge that greeted them. They felt that a soundtrack was playing for them, although they couldn't agree on what kind of music it was.

Marty Was A Very Clever Rooster Indeed

There stood on the chain-link fence behind the hardware store a real fine rooster named Marty. He would stand perfectly still and make the passing people of our town wonder if he was real or not. He never made noise, not even when the daylight first hit him. He was a real joker this one.

The Higgins twins came by one day and stared at Marty real closely trying to figure out if he was real or not. From a distance, I could see the twinkle in that wily rooster's eyes as he tried to keep the twins guessing. They looked at each other and back at Marty and again at each other. They were real confused.

The next day, I met up with the Higgins twins in front of the hardware store. They had seen me watching them wondering about Marty. They had to know whether or not he was real.

I couldn't bring myself to lie to the kids, but I couldn't be the one to spoil the joke that Marty the rooster had spent so much time developing. I guess the twins could see through me because they hurried into the hardware store to buy some wire to teach that rooster a lesson once and for all.

Now, I couldn't just stand by and let something like that happen to a humor-lover like Marty, so I did some shopping of my own. By the time the Higgins twins got to the back of the hardware store to do something mean to Marty, I had set up eleven toy roosters on top of the chain-link fence with Marty. The twins couldn't quite figure out which one was the rooster that they knew was laughing at them behind his clenched beak.

The twins looked the roosters over real carefully for about ten minutes and finally twisted the wire around the neck of the third one from the left. I suppose I should have taken the price tags off the toy roosters, but then again, I never liked Marty either.

Fables for the Clarinet

Vera waited for the Banjo Man to begin snoring before slowly and methodically lifting the covers off her body and quietly sneaking out of their canopied bed. She dared not wake him. He would again want to know where she was going and why. Then the Banjo Man would question her motives for leaving their nice warm bed until, instilled with guilt, Vera would climb back into bed just as he started snoring again.

She silently stared at him as she stood by the door. For quite a while, she had asked herself why she ever married him. They had nothing in common and he had absolutely no admirable traits. He was a terrible liar and, after all their time together, she still didn't know anything about his past.

Vera remembered how he had persuaded her to go out with him the first time by serenading her late at night with songs that would have been quite romantic if not accompanied by his banjo. Maybe she was desperate for male attention or maybe she was afraid of having angry neighbors, but whatever the reason, the Banjo Man got his date. Threats of more late-night serenades made him an increasingly important part of her life.

He had a way of making Vera do or say things that she really didn't want to. Perhaps the extra years he had over her taught him how to control her. His words brought out whatever responses he wanted from her.

He couldn't understand her fascination with the boxes of books in the garage. They were, after all, old and musty and belonged to Vera's Great Aunt Hildy until about a week before, when Aunt Hildy's stay at the home appeared to be permanent. The Banjo Man called the old woman crazy, even though Vera never had a chance to introduce them. He always refused to visit the places where Aunt Hildy lived or was kept.

There were sixteen boxes of books in the garage. Vera had only managed to get through about half after attempting to search through them for six straight nights. The Banjo Man would invariably get out of bed and stop her quest. "A lot he cares about what's important to me," thought Vera as she opened the ninth box.

"*Fables for the Clarinet* isn't in this one either," realized Vera as she turned her attentions to the tenth box. "Maybe the book doesn't even exist."

Despite occasional discouragement, she was determined to find the book her aunt read her during her annual summer stay. Her aunt would read her the book while Vera looked at the pictures and quietly wondered why the stories were different every time her aunt read it.

Vera decided her dreams must have become interwoven with the stories her aunt read her. The pictures had to exist though. The fox at the pawnshop, the sparrow with the machete, and Hiram the Majestic aboard the yacht – they had to have existed. Vera remembered the pictures so clearly. Seeing them again would reintroduce some magic back in her life. The book could take her to a time when everything seemed wonderful and possible – and there was no Banjo Man.

Two weeks before, she had found some old photographs, which took her mind off her current problems, but unfortunately, reminded her of the problems of her past. The photograph of her sitting between her parents reminded her why she was sent off to Aunt Hildy's so often during her early childhood. The photo also reminded her of why she was so anxious to leave home permanently and why she was so vulnerable to the manipulations of the Banjo Man.

Another photo she found was of Aunt Hildy. The woman didn't look like she had all her mental abilities even then when she carried a four-year-old Vera. While looking at the photo, Vera's mind replayed a thirty-year-old conversation.

"What does this book say, Aunt Hildy?"

"That says 'Fables for the Clarinet,' dear."

"Can you read it to me?"

"Okay, but don't touch it. It's not really my book, dear. I'm just keeping it safe for someone who plays the clarinet."

"What's a clarinet, Aunt Hildy?"

"There's an encyclopedia here and I'll show you."

The musical instrument pictured in the encyclopedia enchanted Vera. She loved the sound of the word "clarinet" and she remembered looking at the strings on the illustrated instrument.

"Something isn't right here," realized Vera. "The instrument had strings!"

Looking through the next box, Vera found the encyclopedia and she looked up "clarinet." The illustration was definitely a clarinet but she didn't recall ever having seen the illustration before. Playing a hunch, she looked up "banjo." There it was. The illustration that had enchanted her. The strings glistened just the way she recalled them. But where was the frog? There used to be a frog holding the banjo. Or at least Vera remembered one.

As she opened the twelfth box, Vera thought about her last visit to Aunt Hildy's. It was during that visit when her aunt introduced her to pancakes. Vera recalled that they were served at every meal. Did her aunt really call them "flatpies"? Maybe Aunt Hildy was losing her grasp on things even then.

The next three boxes were opened and scanned quickly. If she was to find a connection to her childhood, it would have to be in the last box. And it was indeed there, as well as it existed.

Vera found a book called *A Banjoful of Lies*. The frog on the cover was playing the banjo like the picture she remembered, except that the banjo that the frog held was less appealing than the encyclopedia illustration. Vera decided that her memory had combined the two drawings.

Turning the pages slowly, Vera found a picture of a prince on a ship. The prince's name was James, not Hiram the Majestic. There was a story of a robin and a worm. For some reason the worm was silver, so it looked like the robin had a machete in its mouth.

Vera read the first few stories. Nothing about them was familiar. Aunt Hildy had never really read anything to her. She must have made up everything. Young Vera wouldn't know the difference anyway.

The stories were all linked by one common trait. There was a banjo involved in all of them. Vera didn't remember any banjos in the stories she was read. There were, however, a lot of clarinets in the stories her aunt "read" to her.

She turned each page carefully and recalled every illustration and how each still held its magic for her so many years later. She pictured her aunt reading the book to her and suddenly stopping. She thought about how every so often, her aunt would put down the book and run to the window. After looking outside and saying something like "Must have been a radio," Aunt Hildy would be depressed for the rest of the evening.

After turning the last page, Vera found a message written inside the back cover.

My Dearest Hilda,

Although I have loved you, I am afraid that our love has run its course. I have decided to marry another, someone closer to my own age, with whom I share a deep love for music. She has introduced me to the wonderful world of stringed instruments and I have given away my clarinet to focus on my expanding horizons. I am giving you this book to help you rationalize all that you think about me. This book has the right title, doesn't it? If you can think of those of us who play music as providers of fables (or lies if you prefer), then maybe you will decide that you are better without me. After all, lies for a banjo are fables for the clarinet."

The message was signed, "The Clarinet Man."

"Lies for a banjo are fables for the clarinet," Vera repeated in a whisper.

"Lies for a banjo are fables for the clarinet," she said aloud.

She walked into the kitchen and shouted, "Lies for a banjo are fables for the clarinet!"

Hearing some rustling of covers from the bedroom, Vera decided to walk into the bedroom and stand by the Banjo Man's side of the bed. She shouted, "Lies for a banjo are fables for the clarinet!"

"Vera, why don't you come to bed and stop shouting?" asked the Banjo Man.

"Lies for a banjo are fables for the clarinet!" shouted Vera. "I know all about you now! Lies for a banjo are fables for the clarinet!"

The Banjo Man sat up in bed and realized that Vera might indeed know about him. He didn't know how, but the words she repeated made it clear that she might somehow be on to him.

"Lies for a banjo are fables for the clarinet, my dear Banjo Man," she said sternly.

"I know that line," he said slowly, believing he could calm her with whatever popped into his mind if he spoke calmly enough. "It's from *A Banjoful of Lies*, one of my childhood favorites."

Vera sat beside him on the bed and stared at him. He would catch on sooner or later. The line was not printed in the book.

The Last Tuba Player

"The Last Tuba Player was a kind man," said the Methodist minister to the twenty-three people who had gathered under sunny skies as if to bid a fond farewell to an old friend. Henderson, the imposing figure standing at the other end of the casket, shook his head. The priest noticed.

"The Last Tuba Player was a gentle man," said the minister as he watched for Henderson's response. Henderson, however, knew when he was being watched and remained still. Instead Johansen, the third best-known drummer in the city, snickered. The minister heard this. There was a pause while notes were shuffled and searched.

"The Last Tuba Player was a man of music," improvised the minister. He paused for a response. None was forthcoming, so he continued, "His music was his work. It was his life."

Someone coughed, but it seemed to the minister to be phlegm-related and not any sort of comment.

"The Last Tuba Player will be remembered for what he gave to all of us," added the minister.

There was a long pause. Henderson looked up at the minister, as did Johansen and the other twenty-one attendees. The minister looked over his remaining notes. There was nothing in them that would avoid a debate in the form of shaking heads or comments, maybe even some louder coughing. He would have to improvise.

"My friends, do any of you have any words to share about the Last Tuba Player?" he asked. There were a few snickers and stifled laughs.

The minister shifted his direction, only getting out, "We will miss him," before some serious throat clearing was heard.

The minister was baffled about what to say next. He stared into space instead and saw a white dove fly out of a nearby maple tree. He turned to watch the dove's graceful flight. The dove, however, did a large circle and the minister found himself completely turned around.

"I must be honest with you who have gathered here today," he started. "It's not always easy to improvise in life – especially with you folks. I can only imagine how difficult it would be if I had to express myself with a tuba instead of with words and prayer."

That was it. The minister struck a note with these words. A silence fell over the gathering and a few people even reached for a handkerchief or tissue.

The minister walked away, down the hill and into his Rambler. He wouldn't know how tough the crowd was that had gathered for this funeral until he heard some of their confessions and learned that more teamwork and planning had gone into the Last Tuba Player's death than into his funeral.

Asparagus Still Unaware

Well, we're not as certain as last round. She stood by the recliner and pacified the moments of spring. It would and not too shortly become what the king had predicted – an all-out walrus.

It was late by regal standards. The pompous and the nail-filing brigade slept. They were lost. It had been close to closing when they started looking for the envelope with the cake. The keys to life's dearest frauds were seated on the bureau nearest the oncoming month.

Was it really September? The asparagus rested – uncluttered and pure. The lack of knowledge kept things stable. A book, a bit of knowledge that could be heard from a carnivorous source could change all that. The waltzer thought and wondered if all the remnants were worth writing about. Could Thursday have all been a mental lapse? Surely, the grapes of returning allegories could be subpoenaed before the lawn's first reconsideration.

It was now up to the last one to close the purpose. "Well done" and applause were an off-chance occurrence. This was to be the day of hiding. Leave me off by the newspapers that fold up in a discovery. Leave me to talk to the vegetables and warn them of plates to come.

Quietly the barber approached the cartoons. With a clientele of curious onlookers, he wanted to appear somber and patronizing. His day was the only day that those of the forks and spoons ever knew.

Jets flew overhead, which proved to be the easiest. Toads in a nearby elevator attempted to hop to the control panel. Life was a second-floor experience to those of us who lived in a skyscraping monolith of wonder (including a cafeteria with lunchtime specials no one ordered).

Think before you react to the day's inner workings. You haven't a clue about the asbestos or the barber or the real hijinks that plague most academies. You have chosen an inner peace on the outer fringes of what we know to be worth a moment or two between the commercials.

I am not Fred. I may be someday if I ever educate the asparagus. Names would become unstuck on my planet and you would have to hold onto whatever sounds floated close by.

Walking with Edison

Edna was walking down the street with Thomas Edison as if their lives overlapped. She was a schoolteacher in the suburbs who never had a tan, not even at the end of summer. She read books that she didn't need to about ideas that would never bring her any closer to the things that people are expected to want. It's not that she shouldn't have read. It's just that she didn't enjoy reading. To Edna, reading was a penance.

If Edna had no plans to be with friends and no date, which was almost always the case, she would open up a book to punish herself. The great majority of weekends and most weeknights found her reading. If she had been given the idea to hit herself with a paddle, she would probably never have read. She could have struck herself with the paddle, after deciding how many whacks were necessary to replace each chapter that would have otherwise been her evening's sentence.

So when the people of the suburbs saw Edna walking hand in hand with the inventor of the light bulb and countless other electronic products that we take for granted in our hectic modern lives, they were more than mildly surprised. This man who had died before Edna was born seemed to be sincerely interested in the schoolteacher. When they stopped for donuts, it was the usually frugal Edison who paid for them.

The theory was put forth among the staring suburbanites that perhaps the gifted Mr. Edison had somehow invented a time machine and was visiting the present as part of a science experiment. The theory was eagerly accepted by the nodding crowd, which was more anxious to answer the second and greater of their two nagging questions: Why Edna?

A suitable explanation was not forthcoming. The suburbanites thought and thought and thought a little harder. Why Edna? Eyebrows met in concern on suburban foreheads. They had reached a consensus easily enough to explain how a man who was dead for several decades could stroll down the street and enjoy donuts, but they drew a complete blank when they pondered why he was with this schoolteacher.

The couple walked down the street and into the bowling alley. The dense crowd of confused locals followed about two hundred feet behind them. Edison and Edna selected their balls and were putting on their shoes when Marconi and Bell approached them.

"The inventors of the telegraph and the telephone," was the whisper that spread through the rapidly enlightened crowd.

Edna bowled poorly although she picked up the tricky 6-7 split, which earned her a round of applause from her three new friends as well as from the 270 suburbanites standing in front of the candy machine. Edison was tired after the second game so the four bowlers left the bowling alley and went their separate ways. By the time the locals, who maintained their two-hundred-foot distance, stepped outside, the only person they could see was Edna.

Two-hundred-seventy people watched Edna enter the library and they stood their ground until she left with some heavy philosophy textbooks. She walked home and read all night, not even acknowledging the crowd that stood on her sidewalk until maybe four a.m. They never knew if she saw them or not. Edna was too distracted by her mission.

She agonized as she turned each page, but she continued reading until every newly borrowed book was read. She had completed the night's penance. There would be more heavy books to be read for many more years to come, but someday Edna would earn herself another miracle.

The First Church of the Narrator

Waldo was suddenly under the impression that answers awaited anyone who gave in to the impulse to enter a religious building. This, he further suddenly believed, was especially true for those such as himself who rarely received such impulses. With those thoughts in mind, Waldo parked his Subaru and entered the First Church of the Narrator one August evening on his way home from work.

Waldo, the only one in the church, sat in a pew at the back. He could hear dignified footsteps in another room. And then it started...

"Waldo, the only one in the church, sat in a pew at the back," said a deep voice that came from the speakers perched high in the corners of the church. "He could hear dignified footsteps in another room. And then it started..."

Waldo's first reaction was to get up and leave. He really shouldn't be there. He had never attended or contributed to a church in his life. Maybe his very presence in a church was some sort of sin. He stood up.

"Waldo's first reaction was to get up and leave," continued the voice on the speakers. "He really shouldn't be there. He had never attended or contributed to a church in his life. Maybe his very presence in a church was some sort of sin. He stood up."

Waldo heard the voice providing an account of his every action, even his every thought. He was scared and he sat back down.

"Waldo heard the voice providing an account of his every action, even his every thought. He was scared and he sat back down."

He stood up.

"He stood up."

He sat back down.

"He sat back down."

He wondered what influenced him to ever have entered this strange church. Whoever heard of the First Church of the Narrator?

"I have," said the voice over the speakers. "In fact, I am the very Narrator of which you wonder. Yep, that's me."

"But you stopped narrating my every move..." started Waldo.

"I was just on a break," responded the Narrator. Following an "aah" that can only follow a truly enjoyable intake of liquid, the Narrator was back at his job.

"He wondered what influenced him to ever have entered this strange church," said the Narrator. "Whoever heard of the First Church of the Narrator?"

"I have," interrupted Waldo. "At least now I have."

The Narrator seemed rattled. The sound of papers being rustled could be heard over the speakers. Waldo decided to go on the offensive.

"'I was just on a break,' responded the Narrator," reported Waldo. "Following an 'aah' that can only follow a truly enjoyable intake of liquid, the Narrator was back at his job."

"Waldo decided to go on the defensive," said the Narrator, trying to regain the upper hand.

"Offensive," corrected Waldo.

"'Offensive,' corrected Waldo," said the Narrator. "Waldo sat and looked smug in the back pew of the church."

Indeed, this was true. Waldo looked like he had mastered this new game and actually defeated the Narrator. Alas, that was just an illusion, for Waldo was silent for too long and the Narrator was able to take back control of the situation.

"Waldo looked like he had mastered this new game and actually defeated the Narrator." said the Narrator. "Alas, that was just an illusion for Waldo was silent for too long and the Narrator was able to regain control of the situation."

There was a pause; an awkward silence.

"There was a pause; an awkward silence," said both Waldo and the Narrator in unison, "said both Waldo and the Narrator in unison."

There was another awkward pause while the previously mentioned footsteps approached Waldo. As he expected, there was a priest atop those dignified footsteps.

"I'm sorry, we need to lock up," said the priest. "You'll have to be going now."

The priest's voice was fragile but there was a confidence behind it. It was as if the priest understood what the Narrator was all about. Waldo stared at the closest speaker. There was no sound coming from it. This priest was able to move about the building relatively unnarrated. Only his footsteps, which added to Waldo's initial curiosity, had been discussed by the Narrator. The priest was at peace with the Narrator. Waldo had been in competition with it.

As he drove away in his Subaru, Waldo had more questions than answers from his visit to the church. In fact, he only had one answer and that was to drive to the beach and contemplate the waves under the glow of the moon.

Somebody Tall Was in the Next Booth as I Waited

Somebody tall was in the next booth as I waited for my order. Perhaps I knew who the person was, I thought to myself. After all, I watch a lot of basketball and football on television. Maybe the person in the next booth was an athlete. As I left, I looked at the tall person more closely.

It was Nero the Axe murderer! I quickly slipped into the night.

I heard a voice calling me as I rushed down the street. I know that voice, I thought to myself. It's a very familiar female voice. I turned and looked. Oh, no! It was Sylvia the Beheader. Time again to hurry.

I managed to find a taxi. I got in and breathed a sigh of relief as it sped out of the area. When I looked at the driver's photo on the dashboard, I thought I recognized him. He sure looked familiar. The name, however, wasn't. I had to ask him if that was really his name. He told me that it was his real name but he had just recently changed his name from Karl the Flesh Mangler.

We went bowling that night and he introduced me to his sister. She and I were soon married. We have three kids and live in the suburbs.

Cosmo and His Wonderdog

"Perhaps, my dear, more dirt would be able to surrender itself to the mop if your mop touched the floor more often," suggested Cosmo to his dear lady, Bella Clara, as she sweated in their kitchen.

"Woof," added Wonderdog.

Bella Clara looked at the top of the mop handle and perused her memory of Cosmo's orifices. She calmed to a point where sarcasm was once again her ally.

"It's very kind of you to spend your afternoon supervising when you could be having fun washing the car," she responded.

"Woof," commented Wonderdog, which meant that the ball was back in Cosmo's court.

"My dear, I only meant to help you," said Cosmo. "Wonderdog and I hate to see you sweat so much."

"Perhaps, if you would give up on your silly plan to market Wonderdog souvenirs, we could leave Wonderdog someplace remote," Bella Clara said with noticeable anger. "And then the kitchen floor would not get so dirty."

"But my dear, don't you remember what happened when you talked me into doing just that in exchange for you wearing the pig ears that August night?" asked Cosmo. "Wonderdog telephoned the authorities and for a while we were looking at some serious jail time."

"That was your fault, Cosmo!" responded Bella Clara. "I saw you slip him the quarter and tell him where a pay phone was."

"Oops," was Cosmo's only response.

"Woof," was always Wonderdog's only response, but he did this one in dramatic fashion.

"Wonderdog, it's not that we don't like picking up after you but, jeez louise, Cosmo is passing up his big chance at Burger King for this strange notion of making you a celebrity," said Bella Clara to the still-stunned Wonderdog.

"She's right, you know," explained Cosmo. "I could have been assistant graveyard shift manager if not for my dreams."

"Woof," offered Wonderdog, and he walked out of the room.

There was a long period of quiet while Cosmo and Bella Clara each replayed the completed discussion in their heads. Before the next round, however, Wonderdog walked by Cosmo and out the front door. On his back was his packed suitcase and taped to his paw was a ticket to New Orleans.

Bella Clara and Cosmo had more arguments in the months that followed. They were also troubled about how Wonderdog was doing. The occasional postcards with dog paw prints did little to ease their minds.

Since the postmarks were all from New Orleans, Bella Clara and Cosmo decided to travel there to find their pal. They were in the city for about three days when some music lured them into a jazz place on Bourbon Street. There they found their old pal Wonderdog.

Wonderdog was on stage wearing sunglasses and playing bass with his teeth. The club was packed. With his backing band, he had the most popular act in town. In fact, after threatening to go to New York to try his luck on Broadway, the club owners quickly made him a partner and even changed the name of the club to "Woof."

Virtually everybody in the place was wearing a Wonderdog T-shirt and some had Wonderdog pennants or Wonderdog baseball caps. Cosmo looked at Bella Clara and he knew that he was right all along about Wonderdog's commercial potential.

Cosmo and Bella Clara left without Wonderdog seeing them. (The sunglasses may have been a factor in this.) Despite not being able to share in Wonderdog's newfound wealth, they found a way to be happy. Cosmo got that job at Burger King and Bella Clara was so grateful that she often wears the pig ears without having to be asked.

Condo Cactus

Something was supposed to be a cactus. It had to be. That's the way things worked in the condo. The other roles had all been spoken for. The penguin nodded in agreement as he attempted a thumbs-up sign with his flipper.

The hedgehog also nodded but his role was less in demand. The Hopi warrior, the helium balloon man, and the porcelain dishware remained quiet and still as their best defense. The cactus was stifled. The cactus was defeated.

When the cactus finally took his place in the corner by the large window and stuck out his elbows and raised his hands, the others all breathed a sigh of relief. It was a done deal.

Eventually, the penguin died. The hedgehog disappeared the day the delivery boy forgot to close the front door. The Hopi warrior was drafted and sent to fight in a profitable war. The dishware showed some chips and was donated to visiting thieves.

The cactus, however, is still there to this day, soaking up the rays of sunshine and surviving on weekly water and occasional Nilla Wafers.

For the cactus, there would be no wavering, no complaints, and no traces of the personality he brought with him into the condo. He traded all that for the respect of those long gone.

Mechanical Wombats

Mechanical wombats made their way to my window as the afternoon drew to a close. They stood on my ground and I stood ready to defend my turf. I was glad that we had a Neighborhood Watch Program and I was hoping to keep them in their places long enough for my neighbors to notice that the mechanical wombats in my front yard were not relatives or friends of mine.

One of them pulled a photograph out of his wallet and made his way to my window. He seemed to be their leader, but I really couldn't tell. He was just another mechanical wombat to me.

The photograph was of me when I was much younger. I was a high school student when they took that photograph. But the picture also showed someone I had not seen or thought about for a long time – Maxine.

She and I were good friends and I suppose as close to lovers as we were capable of in those days. She had a wonderful smile even with the light moustache. She was always smiling. For four years of high school she did nothing but smile. Except of course when she was laughing. And she would laugh quite a bit, too.

She loved to play practical jokes, and she would spare no expense to put people into bizarre situations. I remember the time when she surrounded Mr. Jeffreys with mechanical hedgehogs. Or the time she sent about twenty mechanical oxen into the auditorium during the SATs.

She loved these types of practical jokes although, in retrospect, her ideas for jokes were somewhat limited. At the time, however, we would laugh at anything that took us away from our typical high school routine.

It had been about fifteen years since we graduated and I stood by my window wondering why she had sent a rather large delegation of mechanical wombats to stare at me. I started wondering why this was happening after all this time. I figured that I could understand her better if, let's say, she had sent over a mechanical giraffe or two maybe twelve years ago, followed it up with some mechanical yaks a few years later, and kept up occasional communication with me through similar means through the years.

But Maxine was a tough one to figure out. I decided that there must be some reason for this group on my front lawn. I searched for the deeper meanings of all I knew of Maxine as I walked out onto my front porch and turned on my sprinklers, rusting the whole lot of mechanical wombats.

A day later, I received a call from an animal rights group. They had read an account of my rusting of the mechanical wombats in the city newspaper and wanted to meet with me before deciding whether or not to picket my house. I couldn't believe that anyone would take the time and trouble to stand up for the rights of a bunch of mechanical wombats. These were people I really had to meet.

When they arrived, I stared out my window at them and quickly understood what was going on. They weren't a real animal rights group. They were a mechanical animal rights group. They got out of their cars and stood by my lawn.

I must say that they were a properly dressed bunch. Each of the twelve of them had a bright blue and gold uniform. One of them held a pennant from my high school. That was the tip-off that Maxine was back to her practical jokes again. And once again, my sprinklers proved to be an easy way out of a difficult situation.

The following day, three squad cars of policemen surrounded my house. They were just great! They had bullhorns and everything. I was not to be fooled by Maxine again. When they stood on my lawn, I noticed that one of them was carrying a copy of *The Mayor of Casterbridge*, required reading for senior English back at high school. I remember Maxine and I referring to it as "The Mayor of Castor Oil." I turned on the sprinklers again as an easy way out of an awkward situation. And had they in reality only been mechanical policemen, I would have avoided that night in jail.

The judge looked kind as I pled my case. However, as I spoke about the mechanical menageries created by Maxine both back at school and now, I realized that the judge was probably questioning my sanity. When he sentenced me to ten years for assaulting a group of officers, for keeping a large pile of scrap metal in my front yard, and for contempt of court, I wished that I could somehow find a way to get even with Maxine.

When he stopped in the middle of the next sentence and sat motionless, I realized that this was only a mechanical judge. I turned around and saw Maxine in the third row.

She was beautiful. She had lost some weight and her hair was somehow darker and more attractive. She was truly a beauty now that her moustache was gone.

She took me to her house, which was surrounded by a wide array of mechanical animals. She had a large staff of mechanical servants. When we walked into her library, I got the biggest surprise of all. She had a collection of mechanical me.

There were about twenty mechanical versions of me, all of them replicas of the way I looked in high school. Each was motionless, apparently no longer in running order.

I asked her about these machines and why she had taken so long to contact me. She explained that she had grown tired of being with machines that looked like me back in high school and wanted to see me now after all these years. She smiled and took a few pictures of me. She then had all she needed from me and I could see that she was anxious to get busy on a newer design – *my* newer design. I was driven home by her mechanical chauffeur.

Somehow, I felt sorry for Maxine. Surrounded by machines would surely drive anyone crazy, especially someone with the head start that she has.

Even so, I looked forward to seeing her again in another fifteen years.

ABOUT THE AUTHOR

Steve Pastis is a writer living in the heart of California's Central Valley. He founded, published and edited *The Hellenic Calendar*, the longest-running Greek-American newspaper in Southern California. He created the monthly Word Find puzzle for *Circus Magazine* from 1979 to 1991.

His articles have appeared in a variety of publications including *Greek Accent Magazine* (New York, NY); *Custom Boat & Engine* (Brea, CA); *Baseball Cards* (Iola, WI); *Rock Fever Magazine* (New York, NY); *Mensa Bulletin* (Fort Worth, TX); *Non-Sport Update* (Harrisburg, PA); *Kings County Farm Bureau Update* (Hanford, CA); *The Pop Art Times* (Rockville, MD); *Courthouse News Service* (Pasadena, CA); *The John Cooke Fraud Report* (Santa Ana, CA); *Happening Magazine* (Sunset Beach, CA); *The San Gabriel Sun* (San Gabriel, CA); *The Inland Empire Business Journal* (Ontario, CA); *Brooklyn Parent* (Brooklyn, NY); *Orange City News* (Orange, CA); *Occidental Magazine* (Los Angeles, CA); *Progressive Dairyman* (Jerome, ID): *Parenting Magazine* (Burbank, CA); *Cartoonist and Comic Artist* (Indianapolis, IN); *Cool and Strange Music* (Everett, WA), *The Hellenic Voice* (Cleveland, OH); *SportsAm* (Redondo Beach, CA); *Steppin' Out* (Anaheim, CA); *Good Fruit Grower* (Yakima, WA); *Valley Voice* (Visalia, CA); *Tulare Voice* (Tulare, CA); *Networking Magazine* (Visalia, CA); and *The Good Life* (Visalia, CA).

Want More?

Steve is planning to release new collections of his short stories in the near future. To subscribe to his mailing list, visit NameYourOwnDuck.com

Index